Annabelle Sarne irit
both her English   of
her French uncle.   in
pre-Revolutionar   er,
and when the Co   ot,
Annabelle and   to
England. Their escape is aided by ~~~~~~~~~~ ter
French captain, who vanishes mysteriously.

Annabelle becomes fascinated by her unknown
rescuer, and dissatisfied with her betrothal to Gaspard, Marquis d'Hubert—whom she thought she
loved. How can her heart change so quickly? And who
is the arrogant Englishman, apparently connected
with André, who threatens to deprive her of Sarne
Manor almost as soon as she arrives there?

Unwilling Betrothal

Christine James

MILLS & BOON LIMITED
London · Sydney · Toronto

First published in Great Britain 1980
by Mills & Boon Limited, 15–16 Brook's Mews,
London W1A 1DR

ISBN 0 263 73235 5

Set in VIP Times 11 on 11½pt
by Fakenham Press Limited

Printed and bound in Great Britain by
Cox & Wyman Ltd, Reading

FOR BARBARA MURGATROYD

CHAPTER
ONE

'PARDON, Mademoiselle Annabelle, but your uncle
the Comte desires that you and Milady Solange shall
attend him at once in his private salon.'

'Very well, Suzanne.' With a smile, Annabelle
Sarne laid aside her embroidery and prepared to
rise.

It did not occur to her to think it strange that her
maid should address the Comte's request to her rather
than to her mother. During the four years since they
came to live at the Château de Camoret, servants had
tended more and more to put questions to herself.
Poor Mama! She had changed so much since her
illness following the terrible shock of Papa's death.
Annabelle could remember how Solange had been
before that dreadful night; dainty, exquisite, the pampered darling of English society, a French lady
married to an English gentleman.

At Suzanne's statement, Solange now showed
immediate startled bewilderment, her washed-out
blue eyes filling with anxiety.

'Oh, Annabelle, why should my brother wish to see
us so suddenly? Something must have happened...?'

'Not necessarily,' Annabelle began soothingly, and
Suzanne murmured from the doorway:

'I understand that the Comte and Monsieur Distel
are leaving for Paris again within the hour.'

'There you are, Mama,' Annabelle cried gaily, 'I am
sure my uncle merely wants to wish us *au revoir*, and

tell us how long he is likely to be away on this occasion.'

'Oh yes—er—perhaps that is his reason for summoning us so abruptly,' Solange Sarne murmured, and rose to accompany her daughter.

It was a pity, Annabelle thought, that her mother still clung to this fear of the Comte's disapproval. He must surely have forgiven her long ago for her misdemeanor in youth, otherwise, he would never have come to their aid so promptly after Papa was killed. Mounting the stairs, she was careful still to appear reassuringly nonchalant, but a thread of disquiet was running through her mind.

There had been some shocking tales of late; stories of peasant revolt in different parts of France, of collective violence from villagers turning against their seigneurs, châteaux burnt, women—ladies—attacked and ravished. It was two years since the storming of the Bastille prison in Paris, but the country seemed no nearer social calm. Even the King and Queen were said to be virtual prisoners in the city. Of late, France had become a rather frightening place to be living. Poor Mama was in a constant state of agitation, a prey to debilitating nervous headaches.

Of course, she had never quite got over Papa's dreadful death. Then, at her wit's end and entirely on her own initiative, the fourteen-year-old Annabelle had written to her French uncle the Comte, imploring his aid and advice and forgiveness for past indiscretions on her mother's part. He had responded by sending for them to join him in France.

Entering the salon, they found Henri, Comte de Camoret, standing by the hearth, already attired in travelling clothes. Nowadays, he always dressed soberly when visiting Paris as he considered it foolish to draw attention to his wealth in such dangerous times. He bowed over Solange's hand, directing her to be seated on a gilt sofa, and as often before, Annabelle was struck by the likeness between the brother and sister. Hardly surprising, as they were twins; both short in height, fair-skinned and plump, but there could never be any doubt as to the Comte's air of aristocratic command.

'Ah, my dear Annabelle.' He waved her to a seat also. 'Has Suzanne Dupont told you that I am going to Paris?'

'Yes, *mon oncle*.'

'I may be absent for a couple of weeks. I have asked you here for two reasons; first to bid you both *au revoir*. Also I must inform you that in view of recent happenings in the country, I have decided that it would be wiser for you to return to England, at least for the present.'

'Oh, Henri . . .' Solange began to flutter at once, but her brother raised a plump, well-manicured, imperious hand.

'Be silent, if you please, Solange, and hear me out.' Then, with a trace of impatience, 'There is no cause for imminent alarm, but as a family of noble blood we could be in some danger. Annabelle is now eighteen, old enough to claim her inheritance of Sarne Manor. And as you have told me, Solange, she is also due to inherit a considerable sum of money under the terms of her paternal grandmother's will, so you will not lack for comfort. I shall be much more content, knowing that you are both safely out of France for the time being.'

'When would you wish us to leave?' Annabelle asked quietly.

'Within a few days. There is no immediate urgency.

I believe our servants here are loyal. Even those from outside. The Dupont girl, for instance.'

'Suzanne?' Annabelle exclaimed, an indignant flush rising in her cheeks. 'Her loyalty and devotion to me is beyond question. She is from quite good family herself, as you know. 'Tis not her fault her parents both died of smallpox when she was only five years old, leaving her destitute, so that she had to be brought up by nuns and now must earn her living in a somewhat menial position. I should like, if I may, to take her home to England with me.'

'Certainly, if you wish. It is of small importance to me. But there is a matter that I do wish to discuss with you both.' The Comte's look rather grudgingly included his sister.

'What is it, uncle?' Annabelle gazed at him inquiringly.

'You are now a potentially wealthy young woman, but this does not change the fact that I, as your only male kin, am still your guardian,' said the Comte.

'But of course not, Uncle Henri.'

'I have grown fond of you, my dear niece, but I do not deny that I abhorred your father's manner of life. He was a reckless, spoilt fellow, relying on charm to win him anything he wanted...'

Annabelle opened her mouth to protest and Solange uttered a trembling, unhappy little gasp. The Comte turned towards her.

'I do not want to distress you unduly, sister, but you know that I can never quite forget your early behaviour; Sarne's wilful enticement of you from your home here, your elopement and clandestine marriage.'

Solange's eyes were already beginning to brim with tears. Annabelle rose hastily and crossed to sit by her mother, taking one of Solange's hands in her own.

'Uncle, I beg you not to upset Mama by referring to the past.'

'Some reference must be made. The fact that your father died in the circumstances he did—a pistol duel following cards, when accusations of illicit play were made on both sides, and both participants paid by managing to kill each other—caused, I believe, a scandal that rocked English society to its roots. But several years have passed since that time. I believe that you and your mother will now be accepted again when you return to Sarne Manor.'

'I—I have no desire to enter society again,' Solange murmured in a quivering voice. 'Annabelle and I have lived here very quietly, and I should wish to do the same at Sarne when we return there.'

The Comte nodded.

'Just so, and the manor can prove a refuge for you both.' He added dryly: 'I may yet be obliged to join you there if the situation in France becomes any worse.'

'Oh, *mon oncle*,' Annabelle exclaimed, 'I do so hope you will visit Sarne! Then we may return some of the kindness and generosity you have shown us here.'

The Comte smiled at her, his eyes warming.

'Thank you, my dear, but I shall not leave Camoret to be overrun by the rabble unless I am forced to flee for my very life. Meanwhile, Annabelle, ownership of an estate the size of Sarne, even with a competent steward, is too great a responsibility for so young a girl. I have therefore decided that before you leave France, your betrothal must be announced. You must prepare to be married in your Catholic chapel at Sarne within a few weeks.'

He watched her assimilate the shock of his announcement. Colour rushed into her face then drained, leaving her fair skin a little paler than usual. She was, the Comte thought, a remarkably lovely girl. She had Solange's fragile appearance; large, black-lashed harebell eyes, and delicate bone structure. In Annabelle's case, he knew, it was deceptive. She owned considerably greater strength, both mental and physical, than his sister did. He had grown deeply fond of her, and also had another, particularly private reason to secure the marriage he had chosen for her. He had no heir; Annabelle was his only blood relation.

'One day,' he said, 'when I am gone, Camoret will be yours, to be held in trust for your eldest son.'

'May I be permitted to know the name of the man you have chosen to become my husband?' she asked hesitantly.

The Comte smiled.

'I think you will not be wholly averse to my choice. He too is eager for the union. It is arranged that you shall become affianced at once to my godson, Gaspard, Marquis d'Hubert.'

It was a miracle! It had to be! Without any effort on her part, Annabelle had somehow attained the seemingly unattainable. She was to become Gaspard's wife? His merest glance could set her heart hammering, yet he had always seemed remote. He was older than she by five years and paid her small attention when he visited his godfather. Gaspard, with his air of sophisticated arrogance that befitted his station in life, must surely regard her still as a schoolgirl. In France, marriages were arranged for advancement in wealth and power: in England too, for that matter, but like most girls, Annabelle often dreamed of a romantic lover who would one day sweep her off her feet with vows of passionate love. During the last six months, those dreams had centred on her uncle's godson but she had no real illusions. Gaspard was prepared to marry her for her Camoret lineage, so all-important in France, and in hope of one day owning Camoret. By comparison, Sarne Manor and her English inheritance would seem of little importance. Yet Sarne could provide him, too, with a refuge if the troubles in France caused still more danger to members of the French aristocracy.

The Comte's smile deepened.

'I take it you have no objection to this decision?'

'No, *mon oncle*, thank you,' the girl murmured, eyes downcast.

'As you know, Gaspard's father, the Duc de Serle, retired to Switzerland last year after his wife died.' He paused. 'Gaspard tells me he intends to leave France too until things settle down. He will be content to live at Sarne as your husband until such time as he considers it safe for you both to return to his estate here.'

Annabelle nodded happily, but a small sound made them both glance at Solange. To the girl's surprise, her mother was revealing every sign of agitation; breathing fast, spots of colour on her cheekbones.

'Why, Mama, what is the matter?' Annabelle exclaimed. 'Surely you must agree that the Marquis will make me an excellent husband? Gaspard is your godson too.'

And the Comte added: 'What objection can you possibly entertain?'

Solange gazed up at him nervously, wetting her lips. The ready tears were already threatening to gather in her eyes.

'Oh—er—none, Henri, of course. It is merely that I had hoped ... and Annabelle's father did too ...'

'Well?' rather coldly.

'I—I had thought it might be preferable for her to marry an Englishman now she is to be mistress of Sarne.'

'I see no reason for such a preference. Our godson comes of noble family. I decided years ago that I would wish him to share eventual ownership of Camoret. Through marriage to Annabelle, my only blood descendant, this may be happily achieved. The matter is settled.'

As he spoke, a tap sounded on the door. Gilbert Distel, the Comte's secretary, came quietly into the room. He had served the Comte since shortly after Annabelle and her mother came to France and the girl knew that her uncle thought highly of him. She knew, too, that Suzanne and he were in love but had small hope of marriage, for Suzanne had no dowry and Distel was sadly underpaid for the amount of work he did.

'Pardon, Monsieur le Comte, but if we are to leave within half an hour there are one or two things requiring your attention.'

'Yes, Distel, yes, I am coming,' with a touch of impatience. 'Solange, my dear sister, I bid you farewell and a safe journey to England. *Au revoir*, Annabelle. Distel has made your travelling arrangements. He will return from Paris in a few days' time to escort you to the coast, and Gaspard will surely join you at Sarne within the month.'

'*Au revoir*, Uncle Henri, and—and all my gratitude.'

She received his avuncular kiss on her brow before he followed his secretary from the room, then turned to look at her mother.

'Mama dear, what is distressing you? Do you truly dislike the idea of my marrying the Marquis?'

But Solange seemed unable to answer. She shook her head helplessly, putting up a hand to her brow.

'I—I have a headache. I think I shall go to my room and lie down. Dine without me, Annabelle. Perhaps I may have something later, on a tray in my room.'

'I'll call Suzanne to assist you to undress.'

Having seen her mother into the French girl's care, Annabelle repaired to her own room. She needed time alone to think; to realise that her secret dream was about to become miraculous fact. She was to marry Gaspard! Gaspard, so austerely handsome, the epitome of aristocratic elegance! He did not love her, naturally, but—but he wanted to marry her, and later, he might come to love her. When he arrived at Sarne to claim her, make her his bride...

To cool the flush of excitement on her face, she stepped out on to the balcony overlooking the château gardens. Below, trees and bushes were silvered by early moonlight in the warm summer dusk. A slight movement in the stillness caught her attention. Peering, she perceived the dim outline of a man's cloaked figure standing near the edge of the lawn.

Something almost furtive in the way he moved, staring up at the house, then drawing back into the shadows as if not wishing to be observed, puzzled her. Who could it be, lurking there watching the château in apparent stealth? Perhaps she ought to acquaint her uncle of his presence before the Comte left for the capital?

She was about to go inside and pull the bellrope to summon a servant when she glimpsed another movement. Someone else was slipping quietly across the garden, and this person quite obviously hoped to avoid detection, for he slid from shadow to shadow, taking care to keep out of patches of moonshine.

Annabelle stared, Surely, that second figure—it looked remarkably like her uncle's secretary, Distel. In the soft darkness enveloping her balcony she was scarcely likely to be seen, but she drew back against the wall and stood watching. Distel, if indeed it were he, joined the cloaked man. They talked earnestly for some moments then separated and Distel came hurrying back, slipping between the trees towards the house. It *was* Gilbert Distel. For a fleeting second, by the light from a window, she saw his face before he vanished from her view.

Perhaps it meant nothing of import, but the apparent swift secrecy of the meeting among the bushes puzzled, disturbed her. On impulse, she turned into the room and hurried to the door. If she could catch her uncle before he and Distel left for Paris, draw the Comte aside for a few private words...

As she reached the foot of the staircase, she heard the clatter of carriage wheels, the thud of hooves. She had just missed him. The coach had gone.

Next morning dawned sunny and warm. Solange was still in bed, so Annabelle took her embroidery out on to the terrace. Seated by the balustrade, she could see right across the valley; a view of tilled fields, the wide slow-moving river, and the road leading north west to Paris. If only its dust would become disturbed by flurries, heralding the approach of a carriage! Her newly affianced, the Marquis d'Hubert!

As she sat gazing into the peaceful valley, something drew her attention. Normally, at this hour, the cultivated fields should have been dotted by the bent forms of her uncle's peasants, working the land. This morning no one was at work. From where she sat, she could see a knot of those same peasants standing in animated conversation at the corner of a field. Evidently they were discussing something of import, gesticulating with French vigour, turning now and then to look up at the turretted grey shadow of the castle on the hill. What was more, even at that distance she could recognise the figure of the overseer standing nearby, and he did not appear to be making any attempt to drive the men back to their tasks.

This, more than anything else, caused her to experience a chill of apprehension. Even as she stared, she perceived a stirring of dust along the Paris road. It gathered into a whorl in the midst of which a rider could be discerned, galloping madly towards the village. Embroidery needle poised, Annabelle strained to see in the sunlit brightness. It could not be the Marquis arriving, for he never came without his carriage and full retinue of servants. A messenger, then? From the Marquis? From Paris? What dire news could he be carrying to ride with such reckless, frantic haste?

Even as she stared, trying to recognise the visitor, he turned aside and vanished behind some trees concealing a drive leading round to the back of the château. Annabelle began gathering up her embroidery silks, preparatory to going indoors to discover what was afoot. Then she saw Suzanne Dupont running across the terrace towards her. Annabelle half-rose in an uprush of acute anxiety. The maid's whole aspect revealed desperate agitation. Her round young face was contorted, tears of fright coursing down her cheeks.

'Suzanne . . .?'

'Oh Mademoiselle, Mademoiselle, come quickly!'

'What on earth has happened?'

'It is Monsieur le Comte . . .' The maid began wringing her hands.

'My uncle?'

'Mademoiselle, he has been taken! Arrested!'

'Arrested!' Annabelle gasped, horrified.

'Distel has just ridden in to warn us. Soldiers are coming from Paris for you and Milady Solange. You must escape at once!'

Annabelle dropped her circlet of embroidery on the flagstones.

'Quick!' Suzanne urged 'Monsieur Distel says there is no time to lose.'

Annabelle caught up the skirts of her yellow sprigged muslin morning gown and hastened after Suzanne back towards the open doorway leading into the château's gold salon. On the threshold, she paused, seeing her uncle's secretary standing by the huge fireplace. Distel was a type of northern Frenchman, olive-skinned, dark-eyed, but now his sallow skin had a greenish pallor and his eyes were red-rimmed by tiredness. He was covered from head to foot by white road dust. He wasted no time on civilities.

'Mademoiselle Annabelle, you are in the gravest danger; your mother, as the Comte's sister, even more so. Your uncle has been arrested. A number of soldiers are on their way from Paris now to arrest members of his family.'

'Ah, *mon Dieu*!' Annabelle's hand flew to her throat. 'What is it my uncle is supposed to have done?'

'A couple of days ago, the King and Queen attempted to flee from Paris. They headed towards the army on the eastern frontier, but their coach was involved in a number of mishaps. It was overtaken at Varennes and Their Majesties are being brought back to the capital. The Comte is accused of being implicated in the plan to aid their escape.'

Annabelle uttered a choked cry but Distel went on:

'I managed to conceal myself when the rabble broke into the Paris house, and overheard something of what was being said. Your uncle will be taken before a Citizens' Court and tried. As soon as I could, I slipped away to warn you.'

Could she trust him? Annabelle was remembering last night and his strange meeting with the cloaked man in the garden, but she had no choice other than to do so.

'Oh my good Monsieur Distel, thank you, thank you,' she cried distractedly. 'Thank you for your loyalty. Oh, what shall we do? My mother...'

'Do not be distressed, Mademoiselle. Listen!'

Annabelle had privately always considered Gilbert Distel to be rather a dull, insignificant young man and been surprised by how much attraction he apparently held for Suzanne. Now she was amazed by the cool manner in which he took command. Behind his spectacles, his dark eyes glistened. His voice had assumed a brisk authority. 'The Comte is a wise gentleman. He foresaw such a contingency as this and made certain plans. A closed carriage has been prepared; the Camoret crests already removed. You and Lady Solange must leave at once.'

'But Monsieur Distel...'

'Pardon, but there is no time for argument. Speed is essential if you are to reach the coast ahead of the soldiery. Where is Milady Solange?'

'Still in her room, I think.' Annabelle glanced at Suzanne who was standing agitatedly by the door.

'Yes, Mademoiselle Annabelle, she is still in bed.'

'Go up at once and bring her down,' Distel ordered. 'Wear your simplest clothes and no jewellery. If we are stopped, it will not do to appear wealthy. You may each bring one valise containing necessities, and bring your jewels and any money you can lay hands on, in a separate bundle. I fear you may be forced to bribe your way out of the country.'

'But—but where are we going?' Annabelle faltered.

'To England, naturally. To your own estate at Sarne. There should be a boat waiting for you in a small bay near to Calais. I have already sent a reliable messenger ahead to warn the Captain of your coming.'

'I fear it may be difficult to persuade my mother to leave immediately,' Annabelle began, but he interrupted her curtly.

'You *must* persuade her. Do not waste time, I beg you. I do not know how much time we still have. If Lady Solange protests, you must be ruthless. Tell her we must be gone inside fifteen minutes unless she wishes to lie in a Paris gaol tonight. You *must* hurry.'

'Yes, yes. I see that.'

'You, I think, may travel as yourself; a young English lady returning from vacation in the south. Your mother should pose as an English lady too—your duenna. If she feigns illness and does not speak, no one need know she is French if we are stopped and questioned.'

'You are coming with us?' Annabelle exclaimed, thankfully.

'I shall see you to the boat. One thing; a favour. Will you take Suzanne with you to England? I may not be free to care for her, and who can say what may happen when the soldiers arrive and find you gone? Or what the future holds for France.'

'Certainly, if she wishes to come. Suzanne is my friend and companion as well as my maid.'

'Oh please, Mademoiselle, take me with you,' begged the French girl tearfully. 'I am so very frightened, and I know Monsieur Distel's mind will be so much relieved if he is aware that I am safe.'

'Of course you shall come, Suzanne. I should detest having to part from you.'

'Thank you, Mademoiselle,' the secretary said quickly. 'Now, go please, and bring your mother down. Ten minutes only mind.'

The two girls hurried together up the château's wide marble staircase. Terror for their present situation levelled the position between them and they spoke as equals, panting from exertion as they ran along the corridor leading to Solange Sarne's suite of rooms.

'You must help my mother dress, Suzanne, while I collect a few clothes and our jewels.'

'Yes. And do not forget to bring any money you have. We may need it for bribes,' Suzanne gasped.

'This will be a severe shock to Milady. Let me explain,' Annabelle ordered as they rushed into the boudoir without waiting for a command to enter. Fortunately, Solange was alone, her maid Mathilde having gone down to fetch up a light repast. Annabelle's mother, wearing a pink swansdown negligée and frilled lace cap, was sitting in the huge canopied bed, propped by pillows. The room seemed dim for the heavy velvet casement curtains were still partly drawn, shutting out the flood of late June sunshine.

Annabelle remembered a time when her mother had been considered as dainty as a flower, adored by her husband and pampered by English society as one of its fairest ornaments. In the past four years, Solange had allowed herself to run to seed, indulging herself with sweetmeats, lazing through each long lonely day without objective, drowning in self-pity. Now, she resembled a plush puff-ball rather than a flower; quivering pink chins, curls fading from blonde to ash-grey, sad blue eyes. She was a woman who could not relinquish her troubles. She treasured them, Annabelle sometimes thought rather guiltily, as many ladies will treasure their rings and brooches. She felt a strong sense of protective sympathy for her mother, but also occasional irritation. Surely Mama could try a *little* harder than she did to be brave and sensible?

She started up as the two girls rushed in, saying weakly: 'Annabelle! Suzanne! How can you? Bursting in with such noisy vigour when you know it makes my head ache.'

'Mama!' Annabelle, beside the bed, interrupted her. 'You must rise at once. I do not want to alarm you, but...'

'Alarm me? What do you mean?'

'You must let Suzanne help you dress quickly. There is trouble...'

'Trouble? What trouble? Holy Virgin... where is my brother? What has happened?'

'Uncle Henri has been—detained in Paris.' Coming up the stairs, Annabelle had decided to conceal the fact of the Comte's arrest as long as possible. 'I expect he will join us in England soon, but we must leave at once. Monsieur Distel has hurried back to warn us. Soldiers are coming here.'

'Soldiers? Here? Why? Ah, *mon Dieu* ...'

'There is no danger, Milady, if we leave at once,' Suzanne cried.

'Danger?' Solange turned deadly pale and seemed about to collapse on the pillows, but Annabelle pulled back the coverlet.

'Suzanne, hold your tongue,' she said fiercely.

'There is nothing to fear, Mama, if we go now. Monsieur Distel has assured me of that, but it might be wiser not to waste any time. We must leave for England immediately. Come, let Suzanne assist you with your gown.'

'Oh, what is going to happen? Are the peasants in revolt? Why are soldiers coming to Camoret? Oh, I do not understand what is the matter.'

The ready tears were gathering in her eyes, but to Annabelle's relief she began getting out of bed and permitted Suzanne to start clothing her.

'Annabelle, what are you doing there?'

The girl was at her mother's dressing-chest, tipping the contents of the jewel-case into a chamois leather bag and searching out a fresh nightgown and change of underwear.

'We cannot take much with us, Mama. There is no time to pack all our things.'

'We *are* in danger!' Solange gasped 'Are the soldiers coming to arrest us? Why? Why? Where is my brother? Where is Henri?'

She showed incipient signs of throwing a fit of hysterics, and burst into tears. Annabelle caught her breath, then remembered the secretary's command that she must, if necessary, be ruthless.

'Mama, pull yourself together!' She forced herself to sound sharp. 'Uncle Henri has been arrested and we are in danger, but we shall be safe if we go now. Go downstairs with Suzanne. I shall follow in a moment when I have been to my room to collect some belongings.'

She did not wait to see the effect of her impertinence in speaking to her mother in such a tone, but ran along the passage to her bedroom. This was no moment for scruples. It took only a few moments to tie her necklaces and bracelets in a scarf, and snatch a light cloak from her wardrobe. All else must be left. She could obtain new clothing in England. She headed back for the stairs. As she reached the hall, Suzanne ran in through the front entrance, pushing past two astonished footmen. Her face was ashen.

'Mademoiselle, quickly! Quickly! Soldiers are coming along the road.'

Annabelle flew outside. Distel, wearing coachman's clothes, had the carriage door open for her. She glimpsed her mother's terrified face at one window as the secretary seized hold of her arm, almost throwing her inside. A second later, he was on the box and they were lurching away, taking a route round to the back of the château that was hidden from the main road.

The first hour of that journey remained for ever as a nightmare memory to Annabelle. She guessed they had about twenty minutes start before the soldiers reached the château and discovered they had gone. Suppose they were pursued? Surely men on horseback could travel faster than a carriage bearing three terrified women?

They were jerked and thrown about as they clung desperately to their few possessions. Solange was sobbing wildly; Suzanne praying out loud for the Virgin to aid them. Annabelle gritted her teeth, determined not to give way to panic, but every moment finding it harder not to become infected by the hysteria of the other two. She kept twisting round, trying to peer through the tiny rear window of the coach to see if they were being followed, but presently she gave up and concentrated on preventing herself from being thrown on to the floor whenever the vehicle jolted over potholes in the road. Gilbert Distel was driving the horses as fast as he dared, but no animal could be expected to keep up such a cracking pace. Presently their pace slowed to a steadier rate, and the three dishevelled ladies were able to take better stock of their situation.

Inside the carriage it was stifling, for Distel had ordered the blinds kept down to prevent their being recognised. Once outside their immediate area, they were forced to stop several times, for poor Solange was overtaken by carriage sickness. There was no need, Annabelle thought pityingly, for Mama to 'feign illness' in pretending to be her English duenna. Soon, Solange lay slumped in her corner, eyes purple-smudged by fatigue and distress. Suzanne's eyes were closed but her fingers jerked at her wooden rosary beads, her lips moving in continuous muttered prayers.

Annabelle felt desperate anxiety concerning the fate of her uncle the Comte. What would happen to him if he were found guilty of trying to aid the royal escape? A long term of imprisonment? Or—or worse? Might he have to face possible execution? She shuddered with fear at the thought.

Breaking on the wheel had been replaced by a new method, relatively quick and painless—a decapitating machine named after a certain Dr Guillotin, who had warmly commended its 'humane operation'. The mere thought of even that being applied to her uncle's neck filled her with sickened horror. *Had* the Comte known of the King's plan to join the army in the east and bargain from there? It seemed quite possible. Her uncle had dealings with many important people connected with the court. She wondered forlornly if she would ever see him again. She was not especially fond of him. He could be strict and harsh, but she was immensely grateful for the generosity he had shown to herself and her mother. She felt keen anxiety, too, for the Marquis d'Hubert. Perhaps he might also be in danger now.

They stopped at a posting inn late in the afternoon to change the weary horses. The innkeeper looked surly, and Annabelle fancied he eyed them with deep suspicion when Gilbert Distel asked for a private room where 'the young English lady and her duenna may rest and have refeshment'. They were taken into a not-very-clean room behind the taproom and Distel demanded food, and a glass of watered milk laced with brandy for Solange.

Suzanne aided Annabelle's mother to a wooden settle near the empty fireplace, where the lady sank down. She looked very ill, her drawn face sheened by perspiration. The fact that her mother had ceased to moan and complain made Annabelle fearful that she was really ill and the girl felt extremely worried. Suzanne knelt on the floor, coaxing the invalid to sip the milk and brandy while Annabelle stood impatiently at the window, waiting for Distel's return from the stableyard. Presently a serving wench brought a tray of food; some rather stale chunks of pie and watery cabbage, to be washed down by ale from thick earthenware mugs. Solange turned shudderingly away, but Annabelle suddenly discovered herself to be ravenous. She had had nothing since *petit déjeuner* early that morning. She noted that Suzanne also, despite her continuing state of fear, ate all her portion.

When the secretary returned, Annabelle jumped up and hastened to him, speaking in a low voice.

'Monsieur Distel, my mother is truly unwell. May we remain here for some hours so that she can rest?'

'No, Mademoiselle, I dare not risk it. I do not think we are being pursued, but even now we cannot be certain. When Milady Solange is safely on board the boat, she may rest and sleep.'

'Monsieur, do—do you think the Marquis d'Hubert will also be in danger now?' She blushed as she asked the question, and added, looking down: 'We—we are to be married when he follows me to England. I do not know if the Comte mentioned the matter to you?'

'Yes, Mademoiselle, he did.' The secretary looked grave and rather sad. 'I fear that many men of noble lineage may be increasingly at risk, but I am sure the Marquis will have made his arrangements. No doubt he will arrive safely at Sarne Manor in due course.'

With this reassurance, Annabelle had to find what comfort of mind she could. The wearying journey continued, but as the evening drew on, the air became a little cooler. Annabelle raised the blinds to look out over the flat fields of northern France. Suzanne sat fanning Solange with a small fan she kept in her reticule for emergencies. Presently, Solange slept. Suzanne's hands rested in her lap, still holding her rosary, but no longer telling the beads. Annabelle's hot eyelids drooped. Would this exhausting journey never end?

'Halt!'

The ringing command jerked the girl awake as the carriage lurched to a halt. Suzanne gave a small shriek and clapped a hand across her mouth. In her corner, Solange stirred and uttered a frightened moan. Annabelle seized her mother's flaccid hand, whispering fiercely: 'Ssh, Mama. Remember you are my English duenna, Mrs Marshall. Suzanne, keep silent!'

Voices outside, then the carriage jerked as Distel

descended from the driving seat. Suzanne made a tiny whimpering sound. Annabelle found she was holding her breath. Her throat had gone dry. She licked her lips and tried to peep out of the window. In the dim light from the carriage lamp she could just discern a number of dark figures, and a horse snorted nearby. Almost within touching distance, the dull light revealed a pair of jackboots, a glimmer of white breeches, and the sleeve of a uniform jacket.

Soldiers! God in heaven, they were caught! Now, all must depend on Monsieur Distel and herself. Somehow they must bluff their way out. Then, as the terrifying realisation dawned, the carriage door was wrenched open and bright lantern light dazzled her.

'Ah! *Three* ladies! Mademoiselle, to whom do I address myself?'

The voice was deep, speaking in cultured French, but Annabelle, half-blinded by the light, could see nothing of its owner. She clenched her hands until the nails bit into the palms, and with an immense effort after courage, drew herself stiffly upright.

'I am Miss Annabelle Sarne of Sarne Manor, Surrey, in England. I am returning home from a vacation in Switzerland. What is the meaning of this intrusion? Who—who are you? Kindly put that light away from my eyes.'

The light was lowered immediately, but she could still see very little.

'You speak French remarkably well for an English lady.' His voice sounded mockingly amused to her frightened ears 'And who, pray, may these other ladies be?'

'My—my chaperone, Mrs Marshall. As you must see, she is extremely unwell. The other is my maid, Mademoiselle Suzanne Dupont.'

'You will please descend from the carriage.'

'I—I—Mrs Marshall is too ill to get out,' Annabelle protested nervously.

'Only you, Mademoiselle. Descend at once, if you please.'

Reluctantly, the girl gathered her cloak about her and prepared to alight.

'What do you want of me?' Despite her determination to be brave and dignified, her voice shook and she swallowed hard.

'You have nothing to fear. You will not be harmed,' said the voice in the darkness. Annabelle drew a deep breath.

'Monsieur Distel? Where is my driver?' She strove to sound haughty but her voice cracked in her dry throat.

'He has gone.'

'*Gone*?' She was thunderstruck.

'He—removed himself into the forest, Mademoiselle, when the carriage stopped.'

'Distel has deserted us!' She was horrified. Within the coach, Suzanne uttered a choked cry and burst into noisy weeping.

The French officer cleared his throat and spoke sharply to one of the dim forms standing near.

'Gârot! Take the carriage box and drive Mademoiselle Sarne's—duenna and maid to the place I instructed you.'

'*Oui, mon capitaine.*'

'Where are you taking them?' Annabelle turned with some intention of scrambling back inside the coach but a hand like a vice gripped her arm and swung her round.

'You, Mademoiselle, will stay with me. Do not be alarmed. They will be perfectly safe. Gârot has orders

to drive them to the beach close by, where a boat will
convey them out to my sloop.'

'Y—your sloop? Who are you? What do you want?'
Panic was threatening to engulf her.

'A few moments of your time, that is all. I repeat,
you have no need to be afraid.'

The carriage rolled forward, disappearing into the
denser darkness of the woods. Despite his reassurances, Annabelle gave a cry of alarm.

CHAPTER
TWO

'Hush, Mademoiselle. In a very short while, I assure you, you will be reunited with your companions.' The man's voice sounded perfectly cool and calm. 'Now, your hand, if you please, in case you stumble. *We* shall proceed to the beach on foot.'

To her utter astonishment, he reached for her hand and began drawing her along the track. His felt strong, warm and sinewy, but when she tried to snatch hers away, he only gripped it more tightly. He was much taller than she, and his outline in the summer darkness revealed a powerful breadth of shoulder.

'This way, Mademoiselle.'

In his other hand he held the lantern to light their path. As he drew her forward, he remarked in a conversational tone: 'My men will remain on guard here until my return, so we need not fear pursuit. I am certain your mother will soon recover once she is on board ship and comfortably settled in her cabin.'

Annabelle felt quite dazed. *Your mother*! He had said: 'Your mother', so he knew that Mrs Marshall, the duenna, was pure fiction. But who was he, and what did he want of her? She hung back, trying to pull free of his grasp.

'Sir, I am at a total loss to understand any of this. Who are you? Are you the captain of the boat that is to take us to England? The boat Monsieur Distel spoke of to me? Where has Distel gone? How do I know I can trust you?'

He gave a soft low laugh.

'What a catechism, Mademoiselle. Well, I shall do my best to answer your questions. One, you may call me *Le Capitaine Francais*. Two, the boat belongs to—some friends of mine. I am not *that* Captain. The ship's master goes by the name of Strode, and it is he who will take you to England. Safely, I trust. As to your final query, you must make up your own mind about that, Mademoiselle Annabelle Sarne.'

'But—but where are you taking me like this, and why?'

'To the beach, as I said. By the time we arrive, the rowing-boat should be back to carry you aboard. Why are you and I here together? Well, let us say, that for reasons of my own, I wished to discover what manner of girl you are.'

'You wished to...' Sheer amazement stopped Annabelle in her tracks. 'And why, pray, should that be any concern of yours, whoever you may be?' she demanded in heated tones.

He chuckled again.

'As I said, I have my reasons. I am pleased to find that you appear to possess a certain brave spirit. Also, I observed by the light from my lantern when I first saw you in the carriage, that you are a very beautiful young lady indeed.'

'Oh....' Annabelle caught her breath in a gasp. 'I—I—how dare you speak to me so? I would have you know, sir, that I am betrothed, and if my fiancé were to hear you speaking to me with such—such insufferable——'

'Intimacy?' Again he laughed. 'So—you are betrothed. To the Marquis d'Hubert, I must assume? And your "fiancé",' mockingly 'permits you to gad about France unescorted in these dangerous times?'

'We were not "gadding about France",' Annabelle exclaimed furiously. 'And he—he did not even know we were leaving Camoret today. In any event, I was not unescorted. My maid and my mother were with me, and so was Monsieur Distel.'

'Ah yes. The Comte de Camoret's excellent secretary. We must not forget him, must we? We owe him a great debt, do we not?' His tone was mildly bantering. 'Mademoiselle, take care! The path slopes quite steeply here. You almost tripped then.'

Annabelle felt totally bewildered. How could he know so much regarding her affairs? Unless—unless someone had told him? She said sharply, 'Where has Monsieur Distel gone? Do you know? Are you acquainted with him? Why should he leave us so suddenly, without a word?'

'How should I know?' innocently. 'He absented himself before my men could stop him, did he not? Perhaps he has gone back to Paris to devise a plan to aid your unfortunate uncle the Comte.'

His voice was bland, but some inflection in it made her think he was smiling, and his remark concerning the Comte infuriated her. All her fear and angry suspicion flared up. Was he their enemy, and about to try and trap her into admissions regarding her uncle? She stood still.

'Sir, I demand that you tell me your name at once, and show me your face. The French Captain! That means nothing. How do you know so much about my affairs? I insist that you tell me who you are and why you wanted to meet me?'

'I fear my name will mean little to you. It is André. As for revealing my countenance—that might not be wise at this moment. I am a man of mystery, Mademoiselle. For the moment, you must accept that. Besides, look before you. We are almost at the beach.'

Furious with bewildered frustration, Annabelle glanced ahead and saw a glimmer of silvery light between the trees—moonshine sparkling on a ripple of waves. As they emerged from the woods, she could just discern the shape of a fairly large boat some distance out in the bay, and hear the plash of oars. A rowing-boat was approaching the shore. A slight breeze had sprung up.

'Ah! Your transport, I believe,' murmured her companion. 'You will soon be safely aboard and restored to your Mama's anxious arms.' Swiftly, he lifted her hand. She felt the warmth of his mouth pressed against her palm, and he closed her fingers on the kiss. Annabelle gave a gasp, snatched her hand away and tried to reach for the lantern, but he stepped back among the shadows, dowsing the flame.

'*Au revoir, ma belle. Bon voyage.*' His voice floated to her quietly from under the trees, and then, quite clearly, she heard the English words: 'Until we meet again in England.'

'Monsieur ...' But a chuckle from the darkness was all that answered her and the rowing-boat was already grounding on the beach. Another voice hailed her softly in English.

Annabelle's arrival on board the sloop was greeted with hysterical joy by her mother and Suzanne. Both had made up their minds that she had been kidnapped, either to be ravished, or taken to Paris as some kind of hostage. Reassurances on the part of Captain Strode had done nothing to allay their terrors. Solange was already in one of the bunks, and when Annabelle entered the cabin she struggled to sit up, arms outstretched and tears streaming down her face.

It took both girls some time to calm her. The description of Annabelle's conversation with the French Captain had them all at a loss, but Solange was vehement against Gilbert Distel for 'running away at the first sign of danger', as she put it. She soon had Suzanne weeping again.

Presently food and wine were brought to them, but when Annabelle asked to see the Captain, she was told he was too busy. The boat was under way, moving sluggishly in a light wind.

When they had finally soothed Solange to sleep, the two girls crept into the adjoining cabin to converse in whispers. Suzanne was in worse shape than her young mistress, for Distel's apparent desertion had been a devastating shock. Her face was puffy with crying, her usually mischievous brown eyes drowning in woe. As soon as they were alone, she turned to Annabelle, both hands held out in supplication.

'Oh, Mademoiselle, what do you think? Do you believe he ran away? He is not a coward; I cannot believe it of him. Did he not ride with quite reckless haste to warn us and aid our escape from Camoret before the soldiers could arrive? Why should he desert us now?'

'It is hard to understand,' Annabelle said. 'I would not think Distel cowardly either. It all seems most strange.'

'And now I must go to England without knowing what has become of him,' wept Suzanne. 'Oh, shall I ever see him again? I do not even know if I *wish* to see him after his extraordinary behaviour.'

'It *is* extraordinary, so perhaps we should not judge him as yet. Perhaps he will write to you soon and offer an explanation. Meanwhile, you must try to be brave and patient, dear Suzanne. Have faith in him until you have definite reason to believe otherwise.'

'Oh, Mademoiselle, thank you,' the poor girl said tremulously. 'You give me hope and comfort. I will try to be brave.'

'I fear our troubles are not yet over.' Annabelle sighed. 'Mama is not at all well. I think we shall both be kept fully occupied caring for her. Oh, how I wish I could think of a way to help my uncle.'

After helping her young mistress to disrobe, Suzanne returned to sleep on a pallet in the other cabin in case Solange needed assistance during the night. Annabelle lay in her bunk, rocked by the sloop's slow motion and listening to the unaccustomed sounds of a ship at sea. Usually she lulled herself to sleep with thoughts of the Marquis d'Hubert, remembering every look and smile he had ever bestowed on her. Tonight, she gave him not a single thought, puzzling over that mysterious man the 'French Captain'. She had not told her mother or Suzanne of the manner in which he had kissed her hand, or that last softly-spoken English sentence.

'Until we meet again in England.'

And that kiss! Her palm tingled at the memory. How *dared* he? That had been no formal gesture of farewell. He had known she was betrothed, but that kiss had been like—like the kiss of a lover. How could he hope to 'meet her again in England'? Why had he wished to find out 'what manner of girl' she was? It was all intensely intriguing and strange.

Annabelle's prognostication that their troubles were not ended proved true. The crossing was slow, but despite its smoothness, by the time they sailed into Dover harbour, Solange was in a state of complete nervous collapse. Obviously they could not continue their journey into Surrey. They must remain for some days at the Dover inn where rooms had been booked for them, and a doctor was called in.

Before leaving the boat, Annabelle was granted an interview with Captain Strode and she was deeply disappointed when he politely but firmly refused to tell her anything further regarding the identity of the French Captain. It was evident that any attempt to press the matter would have meant extreme discourtesy on her part. All she could do was thank him with much sincerity for their safe deliverance. Leaving the sloop, however, she remembered to look for the name painted on the prow. It was *The Swift*.

Two days later when her mother seemed sufficiently recovered to be left in Suzanne's charge for an hour, Annabelle went out for a stroll. Her walk took her in the direction of the harbour, but the sloop had gone.

After a few days, the physician pronounced Solange fit to travel and they set off in a hired carriage for Surrey. It felt very strange, Annabelle thought, to be returning after four years' absence, knowing that she came back as mistress of the manor; a position her mother seemed only too happy to relinquish in favour of her only child.

Annabelle had been brought up at Sarne, for after her father married, her widowed grandmother had continued to rule at Sarne. Michael and his French wife had occupied one wing.

Annabelle had loved her father very much, for it was true that he had possessed great charm; but she was older now, and she could accept her uncle the Comte's verdict that Michael Sarne had also been a spoilt and reckless man. He had been spoilt by his own

mother, but she had had enough perception to recognise that his weaknesses might lose him his heritage,
so she had entailed Sarne for her granddaughter.

Annabelle loved Sarne, so peaceful and serene in its
country setting, and far from the increasing daily
terrors and tensions of revolutionary France. She had
often felt homesick: now, she looked forward to the
day when the Marquis d'Hubert would arrive and, she
could experience the delight of showing him her
home; the gracious house built at the time of the
Restoration, the yew walks, rose gardens, the little
iron bridge spanning a stream where willows trailed
green tresses in clear water. And the tiny chapel,
standing apart from the house near a small lake surrounded by beech trees. The Sarnes had originally
been Irish Catholics, and in a slightly more tolerant
age retained their faith.

A message had been sent ahead to warn of their
impending arrival and when the carriage drew up on
the piece of circular gravel before the house, the steward, Proudfoot, and his wife came out to greet them.
Mrs Proudfoot's rosy face beamed with joy, for she
had been Annabelle's childhood nurse and was now
the manor's housekeeper.

'Oh my dear soul,' she cried, clasping the girl to her
bosom, 'we have been that worried about you, young
mistress, with all the dreadful tales one hears of the
way those Frenchies are behaving! Oh, Milady,' she
curtsied to Solange. 'You poor poor thing, how poorly
you look! Come indoors, you're quite safe now.
Proudy will take care of you.'

'Ah, *ma chère* Proudy, how good it is to see you
again,' murmured Solange.

'Proudy, this is Suzanne Dupont, my dear companion,' Annabelle said. 'She speaks little English as yet,

so I wish you to be as kind to her as I know you can be. She has had a distressing time and is much concerned for the safety of the Frenchman to whom she is betrothed.'

'Such goings on as there seem to be 'cross the Channel! Don't you worry, Miss Annabelle, Proudfoot and me will look after her. Er—may I ask, with no wish to upset you since the message you sent from Dover was indeed a shocking one—is there news of you poor uncle, Mounseer the Comte?'

'None, and I cannot discuss it now.' Annabelle glanced in the direction of her mother's drooping figure. 'But tomorrow I intend writing to London to seek help and advice.'

The very first thing Annabelle did next day was to sit at the escritoire in the morning-room and write to the Foreign Office, imploring that someone might intercede on the Comte's behalf. She despatched her appeal by special messenger then summoned the steward and set about questioning him regarding the condition of the estate. Proudfoot had managed Sarne since before she was born, and there was nothing he did not know about the workings of the manor, but he seemed surprised by her inquiries. Soon, the reason for his apparent reluctance to answer her became clear.

'I can assure you, Miss Annabelle, that all is going on as it should be. But such business affairs are hardly suitable for a young *lady* to be worrying her pretty head over.'

'Indeed, Mr Proudfoot, all this time while I have been in France, I have had no anxiety concerning affairs here, for I knew that with you in charge, Sarne would practically run itself. 'Tis merely that now I own

it all, I am interested in every aspect of the place.
However, I dare say that you will be pleased to learn
that soon,' she looked down modestly, 'Sarne will
have a new master.'

'A—a new master, Miss?'

'I am betrothed, Mr Proudfoot, to a French nobleman. None other than the Marquis d'Hubert, a leading member of the French aristocracy. I—I
confidently expect his arrival here within a week or
two, and then our nuptials will be arranged.'

She glanced up and was surprised to observe a look
of scandalised horror on the steward's face.

'Are you not pleased that Sarne is to have a master
again?' she asked a trifle sharply.

'Oh, well, yes, Miss Annabelle,' mumbled the old
man ''Tis just somewhat of a—a surprise, you see, to
think of you marrying a Frenchy. Er—Mrs Proudfoot
and me, we did always think you'd wed an English
gentleman.'

'I see nothing wrong. I am half French myself.'

'Yes, Miss. Beg pardon if I seem a bit put out.'

'I am sure you will find the Marquis an excellent
master,' Annabelle said rather coldly. 'Now, kindly
send your wife to me. I must give her instructions to
prepare the west wing against the Marquis's likely
arrival.'

It was such a relief to be safe in England, and
Annabelle felt she might have been perfectly happy if
only her uncle were safe too. Also, Solange's health
continued to give her cause for worry. It was natural
that her mother should be distressed concerning the
fate of a twin brother, but after some days Annabelle
decided that there was another çause for her mother's
obvious nervous anxiety. Solange looked positively
haunted, starting at unexpected noises outside, paling

when a servant entered the room as if she expected imminent dire news.

One morning, when they were in the garden, they saw a post-boy riding up the drive. Annabelle thought her mother was about to faint, but he only brought a note from the London lawyer requesting an interview within the next two weeks. When the answer came to Annabelle's letter concerning the Comte, Solange actually appeared less distressed, although it was courteous but quite uncompromising. The Minister for Foreign Affairs sympathised with Miss Annabelle Sarne and her mother regarding the plight of the Comte de Camoret, but there was nothing the British Government could do. What was happening to the French nobility at present must be of concern to all, but it was an internal matter and France herself must find the solution.

Annabelle crushed the letter angrily in her hand. It seemed plain that no help was to be forthcoming from that quarter. Solange shed a few more tears but quickly recovered when she found they were having her favourite mushroom soufflé for luncheon, followed by strawberries whipped in cream and topped by meringue. Annabelle was forced to conclude that something other than the Comte's unhappy state was worrying her mother. She resolved to find out what was in Solange's mind, but waited for an opportunity when they were alone.

They were sitting in Solange's boudoir one afternoon, sorting embroidery silks for a firescreen that Annabelle had chosen to make, when the sound of carriage wheels caused the girl to drop the multi-coloured strands, exclaiming, 'Oh, Mama, that sounds like a carriage. Do you think—can it be the Marquis at last arriving from France?'

To her startled amazement, her mother turned pale, and put a fluttering hand to her breast.

'Mama, what is the matter?' Annabelle jumped up. 'You look almost about to swoon. Shall I call Suzanne?'

'No, no. Look out of the window. See who it is.' Solange blinked nervously. '*Mon Dieu*,' she muttered to herself. 'If it is indeed the Marquis, what shall I tell him?'

'It is not,' Annabelle said in a disappointed tone from the window. 'It is a total stranger. Someone quite unknown to *me*, anyway.'

'A—a stranger? What is he like? Tall? Dark? Fair?' Solange looked even more frightened.

'He has gone inside. Tall. Darkish, I think. I saw his face for only a moment. Oh ...' Annabelle's own hand flew to her mouth.

'Of whom did he remind you? Tell me, tell me.' Her mother was leaning forward, every line of her body expressing urgent agitation.

'He reminded me,' Annabelle said in a low voice, 'of—of that person of whom we never speak. The one whom my father ...'

She stopped, for Solange had fallen back against the cushions, her lips shaking.

'Oh, heaven help me! It has happened. He has come.'

'Who has come? Mama, what are you talking about?' Annabelle exclaimed, then, as Solange merely lay there staring at her with scared, washed-out eyes, she went and sat beside her and took her mother's hand. 'Mama, dearest, do not look so upset. There is nothing to fear, I am sure, now we are in England. Who is this man? Why has he come here? You know, we are not really two defenceless females.

Gaspard will soon be joining us—in a very few days, I am sure. Once we are married, he will take care of us both.'

'Oh, Annabelle,' cried Solange, beginning to weep in earnest, 'I do not know how to tell you, but I must. You—you cannot marry the Marquis d'Hubert.'

Annabelle gazed at her mother's pink and puckered face.

'*Cannot* marry Gaspard?' she repeated slowly, unbelievingly.

'*Non, ma chère*. It is entirely impossible,' wept Solange.

'But why not, Mama, why not?'

'B—because,' sobbed her mother, producing a wisp of lace with which to dab at her eyes, 'I—I never dared tell your uncle, my brother, but—but you are already promised to Another; someone with prior claim.'

'Prior claim?' Annabelle could only repeat foolishly, staring at her.

'Yes. Be—before your poor papa met his untimely end, he—he arranged for you to marry the son of Sir Julian Lockwood. And you must, Annabelle, you must, or we shall lose our home. We shall lose Sarne Manor, our only refuge, and everything it contains. And you will lose your grandmother's fortune.'

CHAPTER
THREE

IN the blank silence that followed her mother's astounding statement, Annabelle heard footsteps outside in the passage. Someone tapped on the door and Suzanne came in.

'Pardon, Mademoiselle, but there is a gentleman to see you. He gives his name as Mr Marcus Lockwood, and declares that he has a matter of importance to discuss with you.'

'Ask him to wait,' Annabelle said mechanically. 'Direct him to be shown into the morning-room. I shall be down soon.'

'*Oui, Mademoiselle*. Mademoiselle, is Lady Solange unwell? She looks ...'

'She is a trifle distressed over a—a private matter. Do as I bade you, please.'

'*Oui, Mademoiselle*.' Suzanne curtsied and went out. Annabelle turned to look at her mother.

'Mr Marcus Lockwood,' she said slowly, accusingly. '*He* is the son of Sir Julian; the son of the man who killed my father. He—he has come to claim my hand in marriage?'

'Oh, Annabelle, I fear so.'

'But why? Why? Mama, you must explain it. Tell me everything.'

'It was your father's wish.'

'Papa's wish? That I should marry the son of his enemy? The man whom Papa was forced to challenge to a duel? The man who had cheated him and finally—*killed* him?'

'They killed each other,' Solange murmured mournfully.

'I cannot understand. I cannot understand at all. Why should Papa wish me to marry Lockwood's son?'

'Well, he did not exactly *wish* it,' Solange said in a deprecating way. 'You see, *ma chère*, he really had no choice.'

'For pity's sake, Mama, explain! I shall have to go and speak to the gentleman in a minute and send him about his business.'

'Oh no, you cannot possibly do that!' Solange clasped her hands, looking terrified. 'Have I not told you already that we shall lose all if you refuse him?'

'So you say. Tell me how and why.'

'Your poor Papa did have his failings,' Solange murmured, drooping on the couch.

'*Mama!*' Annabelle sprang up, blue eyes blazing. 'Tell me instantly exactly what all this means, or I shall order Suzanne to send Mr Lockwood away forthwith.'

'Oh, Annabelle, do sit down! I declare you quite frighten me, standing over me in such a way. The sad fact is, my poor child, that your father liked to gamble far too well. The night before he died, he—he lost everything. To Sir Julian Lockwood.'

'He—lost—everything,' Annabelle repeated, aghast. 'But I thought—I thought—I have always understood that Sir Julian cheated at cards and Papa was obliged to challenge him, and then they killed each other in a pistol duel next morning. That is what *you* have always told me.'

'It was not *exactly* like that.' Solange twisted the wisp of lace in her fingers, avoiding her daughter's eye. 'Perhaps, at the beginning, I—I was a little confused—The shock ... losing my beloved husband. I was very ill. You *know* how ill I was,' pettishly.

'Well, Mama?' in an implacable tone.

'They—they *were* playing cards. As I have said, poor Michael lost all.'

'But he had no right to gamble Sarne,' Annabelle cried. 'Sarne was entailed for me.'

'He could not touch the money your Grandmama left for you,' Solange eyed her apprehensively.

'Pray continue, Mama.'

'Well, the day you marry, you are to receive forty thousand pounds, as you know, but—there is a condition attached.'

'A condition? What condition?'

'That—that you should marry an Englishman.'

Annabelle gasped.

'The Lockwood estates were in bad shape, I believe,' Solange hurried on, 'so naturally, when he won that final bet, Julian Lockwood was only too ready to claim Sarne.'

'And so?'

'Well, obviously your father could not give him Sarne. So—so—' Solange's plush chins quivered. 'They made a bargain.'

'I begin to understand. Papa made a bargain that four years from then, when I was old enough to marry and inherit my grandmother's fortune, Lockwood's son should become my husband and claim all?'

'Oh, Annabelle,' Solange spoke in frightened tones, 'it was all poor Michael could do. It—it was a debt of honour. And then he accused Sir Julian of cheating. Before witnesses! I fear he must have had too much wine that night. They fought at dawn. I knew nothing of it until it was all over, and Michael—both of them—were dead.' Tears began coursing down Solange's cheeks.

Automatically, almost absently, Annabelle placed her hand soothingly on her mother's.

'And now,' she asked bitterly, 'Mr Lockwood has arrived to claim his rights?'

'We must suppose so. I have been dreading it for days.'

'So I am virtually betrothed to two gentlemen! But I cannot marry Lockwood,' the girl cried out, 'I am promised to Gaspard. It is arranged. He will be here soon, expecting to make me his wife. Oh, Mama, why did you not tell me all this long ago? And I suppose Uncle Henri knows nothing of it either?'

'He knows you are to inherit money from your grandmother, naturally, but not the condition attached. I should have told him, I know, but I am so much less strong-minded than you are, Annabelle. Henri—may the Virgin save him—may be my twin brother, but he is often strict and critical. He thinks me foolish, and perhaps I am,' she added humbly. 'He despised Michael. He was furious over our marriage and only took me back because of you. He wishes you to have Camoret.'

'He has set his heart on my marrying his godson, and so have I. I want to marry Gaspard, Mama, and if I have any say at all, I shall still do so.'

Solange burst into a flood of weeping.

'Then what will become of us, of *me*? You will lose Sarne, your inheritance, *everything*, and have nowhere left to go.'

Annabelle drew a deep breath and patted her hand.

'Do not distress yourself! There must be a way out when I have had time to seek it. I must delay to give myself that time.' She stood up. 'I shall go to see this—this Marcus Lockwood. Dry your tears, Mama. I will send Suzanne to you directly.'

She found Suzanne hovering anxiously in the passage.

'Did you show Mr Lockwood into the morning-room?'

'Yes, Mademoiselle. He does seem a most impatient gentleman. A few moments ago he came to the door and demanded to know how much longer you would keep him waiting.'

'He shall wait as long as I choose,' said Annabelle in a grim tone. 'Come with me to my room. I must look my best to receive this *gentleman*,' scathingly. 'I shall change into my blue brocade gown, the one with silver embroidery upon the panels, and wear my ruby comb. It was my poor uncle's gift to me on my last birthday.'

'Who is this gentleman, Mademoiselle? He seemed to think you might be expecting him.'

'Did he indeed? I believe him to be something of an adventurer, as was his father before him.'

'His father, Mademoiselle?'

'Sir Julian Lockwood. But I dare say you have never heard that accursed name.'

In the mirror, she saw Suzanne's eyes widen with curiosity, but had no mind to satisfy it at that moment.

'My painted ivory fan, Suzanne! Now, how do I look? Have I an air of dignity as befits the mistress of Sarne Manor?'

'Oh yes, indeed. You look very beautiful.'

'Thank you. Now please go and attend upon my mother. She is upset. Soothe her as best you may. We do not want her ailing again.'

Descending the stairs, Annabelle was still too buoyed up by indignant wrath to feel nervous. She threw open the morning-room door without waiting for a footman to do it for her, and paused on the threshold, hoping she presented a picture of icy disdain to the man standing by the hearth.

She saw at once that he was of authoritative bearing; tall, broad-shouldered, lean-hipped, wearing the clothes of a country gentleman. No town fop, this. He wore his own hair, which was thick and dark auburn in colour, tied back by a navy ribbon. He had none of the Marquis d'Hubert's austere elegance, but there was something ruggedly attractive about his features. He was, perhaps, about twenty-six years old, but somehow looked a man of considerable experience. His eyes were cool and clear, golden hazel, an unusual shade. It flicked across her mind that he owned a strong physical attraction, but she, of course, was much too angry to succumb to that. For a moment they stood regarding each other, then his heels drew together in a bow of precision.

'Your servant, Ma'am. Miss Annabelle Sarne, I presume?'

'And you, sir,' she went straight into the attack, 'are the son of the man who killed my father.'

She noted a flicker across his face, then he answered, giving her a very level look.

'And you, I believe, are the daughter of the man who killed mine.'

They glared at each other. Annabelle was the first to lower her eyes.

'Pray be seated, sir.'

'Thank you, but I should prefer to stand.'

Having offered him a chair, she could do no more than advance with all the dignity she could muster, and seat herself on a small gilt sofa. She was at once aware of being at a disadvantage, for he towered over her. She was determined not to speak, leave the initiative to him. As he simply remained standing, looking cool and in complete command of himself, she soon found the silence unbearable.

'I believe you wish to—discuss a matter of import with me, sir?'

'I believe you must know already what it is.'

Infuriating creature! Throwing the ball back into her court! Two could play at that game.

'Well, Mr Lockwood, I am prepared to listen.'

'*Major* Lockwood, Miss Sarne. I have the honour to hold a commission in His Majesty King George's Army.'

'Well, *Major*, kindly state your business.'

'I should hardly call a proposal of marriage "business". Would you?'

'That would depend upon the circumstances in which it was made.'

He looked momentarily amused, and the touch of humour softened his expression and warmed those unusual eyes.

'In our case, this one can scarcely be a passionate avowal of undying love, so might be termed "business". Advantageous for us both, but I prefer to think of it as the settlement of a debt of honour.'

'Honour!' she flashed. 'You call it honourable for your father to have bargained over my future as if I were a piece of—of merchandise?'

'Allow me to remind you, Miss Sarne, that it was *your* father who began the bargaining; to extricate himself from an impossible situation.'

It was the humiliating truth. She bit her lip, clenching her hands in her lap. 'I fail to see how this marriage might bring any advantage to myself,' she said disdainfully, after a moment.

'Surely, you must, since it will allow you forty

thousand pounds. I have seen your lawyer in London and know the exact terms of your grandmother's will. Marry an Englishman and you inherit all. Your father stipulated that *I* should be that Englishman.'

'And if I refuse to wed you?'

'I am entitled to claim Sarne Manor and all it contains.'

For the first time, Annabelle felt afraid. He held the whip hand.

'You would turn a defenceless widow and her daughter from their home, their only refuge?' she asked coldly.

'You make me out a monster. I have not said I should turn you out.'

'So it is my grandmother's money you want? And you can only win that by making *me* your wife. Do you consider it "honourable" to force me into a marriage that is utterly distasteful to me?'

'I am persuaded you will soon find it less distasteful once you have had a little time to grow accustomed to the notion.'

'Indeed? What persuades you of that?'

'Forty thousand pounds,' he said coolly. 'A great deal of money to relinquish—along with your home.'

She hissed furiously: ''Tis nothing short of blackmail.'

'I suppose it must seem so to you.' To her astonishment, he sounded genuinely regretful. 'Perhaps neither of us has too much cause to be proud of our fathers. I have been forced to sell my country estate to pay off my father's debts. My mother now lives in a small establishment in Town.'

'Surely you could always *win* what you need?' Annabelle's tone was silky with sarcasm. 'Perhaps by using—certain methods. Methods also favoured by your father, I believe?'

He flushed darkly and she took satisfaction in seeing his hands clench at his sides, then he said quite mildly: 'If you were a man instead of a mere foolish girl, I would call you out for that remark. It may interest you to learn that I do not play cards or gamble. My family have suffered enough because of that. But whatever my father was, Miss Sarne, he was not a cheat. He won Sarne Manor in fair game, before witnesses, and I have come to claim my rights.'

Annabelle felt herself going scarlet.

'Oh ...' Impotent fury made her want to grind her teeth, hurl things at that cool, implacable, gently smiling countenance.

'And what, sir, if I tell you that I am already affianced? To a member of the French nobility, someone whom it is *my* choice to marry?'

'The Marquis d'Hubert, I assume?'

'How did you know?' she gasped. 'It has not yet been announced.'

'I have made it my business to learn a great deal about you. Do you really think Hubert will still wish to honour the agreement when he finds you will be penniless?'

Rage made her reckless.

'He will not pass over this challenge to *his* honour, I am sure. He is an expert swordsman; one of the best in France. I would not have even *your* blood on my conscience.'

He gave a wry smile.

'You assume it would be my blood spilt. You might be wrong. I might spike that popinjay you fancy.'

Annabelle felt herself grow pale and struggled to find words. Unexpectedly, he smiled, and the smile brought warmth and a sudden charm to his rugged face.

'Come, my dear young lady, I grant that you find yourself in an iniquitous position for any self-respecting female, but time may solve your problems for you. I am prepared to allow you some to grow used to the idea of becoming my wife—and to send your Marquis packing when he arrives. Always supposing he does not retreat of his own accord.'

'Sir, you are grossly insulting both to me and him,' she choked.

'Am I? Well, we shall see. Meanwhile, I regret that I must leave you again when we have hardly had the chance to become properly acquainted, but duty calls and I must obey. In a week or two, I shall hope to return and find you compliant to my wish. We can be married in September—a golden month.'

'No, we can *not*,' she cried hotly, springing up. 'Major Lockwood, I would rather die than marry you.'

He looked oddly rueful.

'I admit it is a pity we must comply with the arrangements as made for us by our fathers. I had no wish to take a wife as yet, not even one who becomes such a devastating beauty when enraged. Miss Annabelle, I shall take my leave now'—he grinned suddenly with the youthful impishness of a boy—'before you grind your teeth with so much fury that they all drop out, entirely ruining your looks.'

With that parting broadside, he bowed himself to the door and left her standing speechless, hands clenching at her sides as she strove to restrain herself from seizing a large Chinese vase from a nearby cabinet and hurling it after him in most unladylike fashion.

Despite herself, his final remark appealed to her
sense of the ridiculous, and a moment after the door
closed she broke into hysterical laughter, tears running down her face. What an impertinent rogue! But
somehow oddly fascinating. Angrily, she was forced
to admit to herself that he had not turned out to be at
all what she had imagined. She had thought she would
find him easy to dismiss. A man of determination, she
realised now. One who, under certain circumstances,
might prove ruthless. It piqued her to know that
neither he nor the Marquis really wished to wed her
for herself, though Lockwood thought her 'a devastating beauty'.

Doubtless, she thought cynically, he would consider
good looks an additional asset in a wife, but it was
evident that he gave not one single thought to her
feelings. She burned afresh, remembering his blunt
remarks, rather too close to the bone for comfort.
What *would* Gaspard's reaction be, once he found out
that there would be no English inheritance for him to
share? There was still Camoret, of course. No small
inducement, unless the *canaille* broke in and ruined it
first.

Oh, her position was indeed 'iniquitous', but what
could she do? Should she try and send a message to
France, to the Marquis, imploring his aid? Yet if he
came, set upon claiming and defending her, in all
probability, the confrontation with Lockwood *would*
end in bloodshed. The thought appalled her.

When she finally went upstairs, Solange was no
help. She asked to be told everything that had passed
in the morning-room, then before Annabelle could
begin telling her, demanded to know why the Major
had not been invited to stay for luncheon and meet
herself.

'It is most improper for him to pay addresses to you directly, *cherie*, without even having met your mother.'

'He was not "paying addresses". He came to discuss the issue with me and make his viewpoint clear. That, he certainly did.'

'He will hold you to the bargain?'

'He means to try, although I have not yet said I will marry him.'

'Annabelle! You must! Would you have your mother cast out homeless in a foreign country?'

'England is not a foreign country.'

'It is to me! We cannot go back to France. Oh, what is to become of me?' Solange wailed. 'The Marquis has no real claim on you. Your betrothal is not official.'

'Oh, Mama, he has a claim. My uncle had arranged it. Perhaps Gaspard will not mind losing Grandmother's fortune. He is reasonably wealthy. Perhaps he will not think the forty thousand pounds of much importance.'

'Forty thousand English pounds not important!' gasped Solange. 'My dear child, you must not let your penchant for Gaspard blind you to reality. Oh, what a stewpot of fish we are in! It has given me such a headache. Send for Suzanne. I shall take a powder and lie down. What have I done to deserve so many afflictions?'

Annabelle felt that the afflictions were rather more hers than her mother's. She had to make the decisions. Whenever difficulties arose, all her mother did was plead ill-health and retire from the battleground. She was deeply hurt at Solange's complete lack of consideration for her feelings and wishes. With Solange once again prostrated, Suzanne in attendance laying cool cloths on her brow, Annabelle dined alone. Afterwards she decided to walk down to the priest's house near the chapel. Perhaps if she confided her problems to him, he might give her advice and comfort. He had been her mentor since early childhood and was ageing now, but he had held a Mass of Thanksgiving for their safe deliverance on the day after their return from France.

Father Martin had lived in the tiny two-roomed stone cottage since she could remember; a semi-recluse who spent his time in meditation, reading, and writing treatises. As she crossed the lawn, heat-lightning was flickering on the horizon. It was very hot and humid again; a storm might cool the air.

She tapped on the cottage door, but it did not open immediately. As she stood waiting, she thought she heard a scuffling within and the mutter of voices. She was about to knock again when the door swung inward and the old priest peered round it, candle held aloft.

'Ah, good evening, my daughter. Come inside.'

'I hope I am not disturbing you, Father?'

'Of course not. I was reading.'

She stepped into the simple little room, sparsely furnished with two wooden-backed chairs, a table strewn with papers, bookshelves round the walls.

'Be seated, my child. A glass of wine with me?'

'No, thank you, Father. I have just dined.'

It was then she noticed something. On the table between them were two glasses still partly filled with topaz liquid. So Father Martin had already had one visitor tonight. But where was that person? There was but one exit from the cottage, and no one had left as she approached. Yet she was certain she had heard voices. So the guest must still be here, concealed in the other room. Someone who did not wish their presence known. Why?

At once Annabelle felt uncomfortable. The walls were thin. Conversation would easily be overheard. She immediately abandoned all idea of telling her troubles to the priest. But who could be visiting the holy Father at this hour, and with apparent wish for secrecy? It seemed strange, but it might only be one of the servants with some matter to confess.

However, she decided not to linger and sought for an explanation for her coming.

'Mrs Proudfoot tells me you have been unwell, Father? I came to ask if there is anything you need.'

'Thank you, my daughter, but I need nothing.' The seamed old face crinkled in a kindly smile. 'There is nought wrong with me but a touch of Anno Domini, as one might say. How is your mother tonight?'

'Still—unhappy. She finds it hard to be patient in adversity.'

'I shall pray for her to receive peace of mind.'

'*I* pray that my uncle the Comte is still safe and well.'

'Keep faith, my daughter. Miracles can happen. The Comte de Camoret may yet return to his family. Trust in the grace of God.'

'I will try, Father. I think I shall go to the chapel for a while.'

'I believe it may help to calm *your* mind.'

Annabelle left the cottage and followed the path leading to the chapel. She had to cross the tiny bridge over the stream and as she drew near it, could hear the soft bubbling of the water and a delicious fragrance of damp meadowsweet drifted up to her. She leaned her elbows on the bridge balustrade, gazing down to catch reflections in the darkling little river. Overhead, stars were beginning to sparkle, and not far away, a nightjar started its husky purring.

'Mademoiselle Annabelle.'

She jumped and whirled round, peering into the shadows. That voice; deep, caressing. She could see nothing. She must have imagined it.

'Is—is someone there?' she asked nervously.

'Do not be afraid,' the voice said softly in French. In the blackness of bushes beyond the stream she saw a glimmer of white, the movement of a hand. He stepped on to the end of the bridge. She could just see the shape of his French military hat outlined against the sky.

'You!' she gasped.

'Did I not promise we should meet again in England?' the French Captain said, and came forward, took her hand and kissed it. This time his lips brushed the backs of her fingers in a formal greeting.

CHAPTER
FOUR

'WHAT are you doing here?' Annabelle whispered, instinctively fearing they might be overheard.

'I came hoping for chance of speech with you, naturally, *ma belle*.'

'You must not call me that,' she protested weakly, adding: 'I—I thought you were in France.'

'And so I was until two days since. I flew to England on the wings of a bird.'

'The *Swift*!'

'None other, but my stay must be brief. I still have—certain matters to attend to in France.'

'What matters? Why have you come? Oh, won't you please tell me who you are?'

'One who already adores you,' lightly.

He had kept hold of her hand; now, she snatched it away. 'It amuses you, no doubt, to mock me,' she exclaimed in a trembling voice.

'Believe me, it is no mockery.' His tone deepened, sounded wholly sincere. 'Love at first sight is not uncommon. I fell in love with you, Annabelle Sarne, the moment I saw you in that carriage, struggling so hard to appear brave and dignified although your eyes were wide with terror.'

'Oh ...' Her heart was racing. She strove to bring the conversation back to normality. 'Sir, you—you have no right to speak to me so. It is quite nonsensical. I do not even know your full name. I have never *seen* you.'

'Do you not find that intriguing?' Again that note of tender amusement. 'Surely you must consider it exciting to be wooed by a man of mystery?'

She began to experience a mounting anger.

'You come to woo me? That *is* nonsense. But just in case you are serious, sir, allow me to remind you that I am already betrothed.'

'To whom, Mademoiselle? The French aristocrat or the English gentleman?'

'Oh!' she gasped again, utterly taken aback.

In the darkness, he took possession of her hand once more, holding it firmly between his warm ones. She knew she ought to pull away, but somehow she could not. She seemed half mesmerised by his nearness, the atmosphere of powerful male virility exuding from him. He was standing very close to her. Her shoulders were pressing against the ironwork of the bridge's side, yet she was barely conscious of the discomfort.

'Listen to me, *ma belle*.' His voice, murmuring in the darkness above her head, filled her with a curiously hypnotic langour. 'You are in a deep dilemma. I know. I understand. But there is a way of escape open to you. Forget those two; the French nobleman who seeks only for wealth and power through marriage with the House of Camoret, the Englishman, greedy for your inheritance. Think only of me. I, André, love *you*, Annabelle, *ma belle*, my beautiful one, and if I cannot have you, it will spell my despair. Love me, Annabelle. Promise to marry *me*.'

So strong were the waves of languorous feeling engulfing her that she would have slipped to the ground if his arms had not come round her, drawing her close. Her head fell back as she lay against him and then his mouth came down on hers. The ecstatic sweetness of his kiss drowned her senses, leaving her trembling and shaken.

'My beloved,' he murmured, his breath warm on her lips, 'trust me. I beseech you to believe in me. I swear I shall not desert you. I must leave you for a while, but I shall return, and then I promise by all that I hold most sacred that I shall come openly to claim you before the whole world, and make you mine. Annabelle, say you love me. Say the words just once, so that I may carry them as a talisman against all danger when I sail for France.'

'Danger?' she breathed, fear suddenly swooping on her. 'Is there danger—for *you*?'

'None, I swear, if your love enfolds me. Say it, *ma petite belle*. Whisper it in the language of love we both know. André, *je t'aime*. André, I love you.'

'André, *je t'aime*,' she breathed dreamily, and felt the velvet warmth of his mouth on hers once more.

'*Au revoir*, sweet Annabelle. In a very little while we shall be together, I pray, never to be parted again. *Au revoir*, my love, goodbye.'

The darkness swallowed him. She remained clinging to the bridge's balustrade, dazed, shaken, breathless and dizzy with feeling; mingled ecstasy and fear.

Slowly the tumult inside her began to subside. Could this be happening to her, Miss Annabelle Sarne, mistress of the manor? It must be madness, or a dream. How could she have *let* it happen? She had whispered: 'I love you,' to a virtual stranger, someone whose face she had never even seen. His kisses had filled her with a passionate joy, yet she did not know his true name.

Madness! Yet such bewitching lunacy! The most heavenly experience of her life so far! If this were love, then it knew no reason, only rapture and delight—and terror for the beloved's safety. What was his mysterious 'mission in France' that, apparently, necessitated concealment of his identity even from her whom he claimed to love and desired to marry? Was it indeed dangerous? Was his life to be put in peril? His life, that had become, in a matter of moments, so infinitely precious to her?

'André,' she murmured dreamily, 'André, man of mystery.'

How long must she wait to have it all explained? In the meantime she must face reality again; Lockwood and the Marquis, Gaspard, who only a few hours ago she had imagined she wished to marry! Now she believed that wish had been conjured by an adolescent infatuation. *That* had been the dream; a dream without vital breath. As for Lockwood, she could only hate his very name.

A white flare suddenly lit the garden, throwing trees, the chapel, and the roof of the priest's house into vivid relief. Thunder growled: the storm was about to break. Annabelle gathered her skirts and began hurrying back towards the manor house. Her mind was busy; she could think clearly again.

Who was the visitor in Father Martin's cottage? The person concealed in the back room? Could it have been André? Did he know the priest? If so, could Father Martin give her more information regarding her mysterious lover? She resolved to seek him again next day and try to question him.

As she reached the terrace in front of the house, lightning again illuminated the surroundings and the first heavy droplets of rain fell on her shoulders. Entering the house, she hastened upstairs to her room. She longed to be alone, to relive those wonderful minutes spent with André, puzzle and try to under-

stand her own changed feelings; pray for André's safe
return. But when she opened her bedroom door, she
found Suzanne setting out her night things.

Annabelle saw at once that the French girl was
distressed. Her lips were pressed together, and two
spots of colour flamed on her cheekbones, a sure sign
with Suzanne that she was either angry or trying to
suppress tears. When she bobbed her curtsey, her eyes
were downcast. Annabelle stood still.

'Oh, Suzanne! What is the matter? You
look—upset.'

'It is nothing, Mademoiselle.'

'But there *is* something wrong. I can tell by the way
you look.' Annabelle paused. 'Is my mother asleep?'

'I do not know, Mademoiselle. She dismissed me
from the room.'

'Ah.' Annabelle uttered a small sigh. 'You had
better sit down, Suzanne, and tell me all about it.'

'Oh, Mademoiselle, she is quite *impossible*!' burst
out the French girl. 'She so completely lacks consideration for *you*, for your feelings. That is what
makes me angry.'

'In what way?' Annabelle asked quietly.

'She spoke of the gentleman who called here today;
Major Lockwood. She told me that he wishes to marry
you, and that your own Papa had arranged that you
should, and if you refuse ...' Suzanne stopped and
stood gazing at Annabelle rather apprehensively.

'Well? Pray continue, Suzanne.'

'She—she said that if you refuse, he will be entitled
to take the manor away from you, and we shall be
homeless. She—oh, Mademoiselle, she wished me to
intercede with you to do as she wants and agree to wed
this English Major.'

'And what did you answer?'

'I told her I should *never* try to persuade you into doing something you did not desire to do, and—and I dared to remind her that your uncle the Comte had arranged for you to marry his godson, and that it was your own wish too. She became enraged, and ordered me from the room.'

'I see. Well, Suzanne, I know that Mama can be—rather difficult at times. She tends to see only her own viewpoint. But I think we must be patient with her. She loved my father, and has never wholly recovered from the shock of his tragic death. We must endeavour to try and find ways of making her life happier now we are here, in England. Will you help me in this? I am so very sorry she has upset you.'

'It is of no real consequence. *I* am sorry you discovered me in this bad mood.'

Annabelle smiled.

'Suzanne, you are my only true friend, and I must talk to someone. If I confide in you, will you swear upon the Holy Bible,' she seized it from the bedside table and held it out, 'that you will repeat nothing of what I tell you? Especially, vow not to tell my mother?'

'There is no need to make me swear on the Bible,' the French girl answered with a certain quiet dignity. 'Any confidences you may choose to give me, I should never repeat. You are the only person I have to care for in the whole world now. I only live to be of service to you.'

'Oh dearest Suzanne, I beg your pardon.' Annabelle laid the Bible back on the table-top. 'Of course I trust you. I should not have required you to swear an oath of silence. It is true that Major Lockwood wants to marry me, but only to gain ownership of Sarne and the money I shall inherit from my

English grandmother if I wed an Englishman. And I now believe that the Marquis d'Hubert wishes to make me his wife solely for reasons of personal ambition—so that the houses of Hubert and Camoret shall be joined. As you know, lineage is all-important to the nobility of France, and Camoret owns by far the greater ancient prestige. But I have something of far more importance to confide in you, Suzanne,' she whispered, tense with excitement. 'I have met the French Captain again!'

'Mademoiselle! Where? When? Oh, what has happened?' Suzanne's brown eyes lit with fascinated interest.

'This evening, after I dined. I went to visit Father Martin at his cottage. Afterwards I was making my way to the chapel when he—André—spoke to me from the shadows.'

'André?'

'The French Captain. 'Tis the only name by which I know him.' Annabelle bubbled into sudden joyous laughter. 'Oh, Suzanne, I am so wildly, crazily happy! It is madness, I know, but I think I have really fallen in love at last.'

'*Mademoiselle!* With—with him? The French Captain?'

'Yes, yes. Oh, do not be shocked or disapproving, I beg you. Perhaps it is madness. Witchcraft! Perhaps he has put a spell on me,' she added gaily. 'Suzanne, he vows he loves me. He swore he fell in love with me at first sight in that wood near Calais; when the light from his lantern shone upon us in the carriage. You remember? He—he declares he wants to marry me too.'

'Marry you?' gasped the French girl. 'Mademoiselle, you do not know him!'

'I am aware that I do not, and yet—I feel as if I know him very well. He is so strong, and I'm sure he is brave, but he is very gentle too. Oh, I realise that it must seem like lunacy to you,' Annabelle cried with defiance, 'but love is not born of reason. It is an instinct, a—a *recognition*. You, surely, can understand, for you are in love with Gilbert Distel.'

Suzanne sank down slowly on to the edge of the big canopied bed.

'I—I believed I loved him, yes. But it seems that *my* instinct has played me false. I cannot help but think now that he has deserted me.'

'Oh, Suzanne!' From rapturous excitement, Annabelle slipped into instant distress. 'It may not be so. I implored you to have faith in him.'

'It is nearly a month since we left France, and there has been no word. I fear I must believe him false.'

'Or perhaps he has been captured,' Annabelle thought, but she remained silent. No use in stirring her companion to even deeper unhappiness. She seated herself beside her friend and touched Suzanne's hand sympathetically.

'Then try to forget him, if you truly think he did not mean the promises he made you. He would not be worth pining for.'

'I—I know that, Mademoiselle, but it is hard to—to put him out of my heart.'

'I understand that it must be. In time, you will manage it and perhaps meet someone more trustworthy.'

Suzanne's head drooped.

'Perhaps. Let us not talk of my troubles. It is you for whom I am now concerned. How could you possibly marry this—this Captain of whom we know nothing?'

'I have not said that I shall. I do not know how I

might. He swore he would return and claim me, and explain everything.'

'But what of the other gentlemen, the Marquis and Major Lockwood? If you marry a Frenchman, you must lose your inheritance.'

'Is my Captain French? Is he English? I do not know. He speaks both languages with equal fluency.' Annabelle sprang up and began pacing restlessly about the room. 'What a situation! I am virtually betrothed to *three* men, and actually to none. Lockwood? How can I do anything but detest the man whose father killed mine? I am filled with rage when I even think of handing over my home to him. The Marquis? Aeons ago, when I was still a foolish, untried schoolgirl, I fancied myself in love with him. That is all it was—a school-chit's romantic infatuation for the only personable gentleman of her acquaintance. And now, André!' She finished dreamily. 'Oh, tonight I can think of nothing, worry over nothing, but him. Pray that he comes back safely to me.' And in an excess of youthful joy, she spun round the room in a dizzying dance. A crack of thunder immediately overhead half-deafened them both.

'Mademoiselle!' The maid stood up. 'You will develop a fever if you permit yourself to become over-excited. It is growing late. Let me help you undress? I'll bring you a warm posset and put something in it to help you sleep.'

'Tonight I feel as though I never want to sleep again. Only dream; rapturous dreams,' Annabelle laughed, but she came to a standstill and allowed Suzanne to begin unhooking her gown.

'I know just how you feel, Mademoiselle,' the French girl said wistfully. 'But I cannot help fearing for you. How can such a situation resolve itself?'

'I do not know, and at the moment, neither do I
care. But I will be good, Suzanne, and not make your
task harder, I will drink the posset, but only for the
dreams it may bring me,' and Annabelle laughed
again, but with a note of hysteria.

Suzanne shook her head disapprovingly and
hurried away to prepare the soothing drink.

Morning brought a return to sanity, and consequently
renewed anxiety. Annabelle slept late, but as soon as
she had swallowed her breakfast chocolate, she
ordered Suzanne to request the steward, Mr Proudfoot, to attend her in the morning-room. When he
came, she dismissed a footman who had been clearing
away the breakfast dishes for she did not want their
conversation overheard and perhaps relayed below
stairs.

'I am sorry, Mr Proudfoot, to take you from any
tasks so early in the day.'

''Tis no matter, Miss Annabelle, if you need me.'

'Thank you. Will you be seated? I wish to question
you on a somewhat delicate matter. I am certain I may
trust you not to repeat this conversation? Not even to
your good wife.'

'You may trust me, Miss,' the old man said simply.

She stood pleating her handkerchief, unsure how to
begin, while he seated himself on the edge of a hard-
backed chair.

'Mr Proudfoot, are you acquainted with the
gentleman who called to see me yesterday? I mean,
have you seen him before?'

'Why yes, Miss. He is Major Lockwood, the son of
Sir Julian Lockwood, deceased . . .' not looking at her.

'Precisely so. The son of the man who killed my
father in a duel.'

'Er—yes, Miss Annabelle.'

'During the past four years, while Mama and I were in France, did Major Lockwood ever call here?'

The steward shifted on his seat, looking unhappy.

'I—believe he did, Miss. Once or twice.'

'With what purpose?'

'I'm sure I cannot say, Miss Annabelle.'

'Did you allow him in the house?'

'Oh no, indeed. Certainly not. With you and Milady Solange abroad! He did not come to the house.'

'Then where did you see him?'

Proudfoot cleared his throat. He appeared even more disturbed. At last, with obvious reluctance, he answered, 'I believe he came to visit Father Martin.'

'Father Martin?' she echoed blankly. 'But surely the Lockwoods are all of Protestant religion?'

'I'm afraid I don't know, Miss.'

'How very extraordinary!' Annabelle murmured, half to herself. 'Have you no notion why he might visit our priest?'

'No, Miss,' the steward said, not meeting her look.

Annabelle was silent for a few moments, thinking.

'Mr Proudfoot, I regret having to ask you this, but I need to know for certain. After the duel when my father and Sir Julian had both received fatal wounds, was Sir Julian's family left in straitened circumstances?'

'I understand that they were. It was said that Sir Julian departed this life heavily in debt. Major Lockwood had to sell his Hampshire estates. His mother and two young sisters took up residence in a minor establishment in town.'

'Yes, that is what he told me. One more question.

Do you know why Major Lockwood called to see me yesterday?'

The steward's elderly face reddened. He cleared his throat.

'Er—no, Miss. How could I?'

'But you think you might surmise?' smiling to show she was not suggesting any impertinence on his part.

'Well ...'

'Come, Mr Proudfoot, I shall be much obliged if you will tell me anything that is on your mind.'

''Tis just that—four years ago, immediately after your father's unhappy demise, there was a rumour, a strong rumour ...'

'What was that rumour?'

'That some arrangement had been made concerning yourself. That when you were old enough, you would return from France to wed Sir Julian's son.'

'I see. It was a common belief?'

'Yes, Miss Annabelle. At the time I believe it caused something of a sensation in the fashionable world, because of the circumstances.'

'The circumstances that our two fathers had been responsible for killing each other?'

'Yes, Miss. I beg your pardon, Miss Annabelle,' he muttered, looking acutely embarrassed.

'Do not, Mr Proudfoot, for it is the truth. Major Lockwood came here yesterday to remind me of the agreement.'

'But the day after you arrived from France, Miss, you told me you had become betrothed to a French gentleman.'

'Certainly I did. The Marquis d'Hubert is my uncle the Comte de Camoret's choice for me. So it would seem, Mr Proudfoot, that I am betrothed to two gentlemen at one and the same time.'

'Dear me. An extremely awkward predicament, Miss Annabelle.'

'It is, is it not?'

'May I take the liberty, Miss, of inquiring which gentleman you propose to honour with your hand?'

'You may, but I cannot answer. Doubtless, time will provide some solution.'

As the steward left, Solange trailed into the room wearing a dove-grey negligée trimmed by ruffles of black lace at wrists and throat. Annabelle regarded her in some astonishment. She recognised it as a copy of one of her mother's half-mourning gowns left behind in France. Since their return to Sarne, they had kept the seamstress busy with orders for whole new wardrobes as well as several dresses for Suzanne, who owned nothing. Lady Solange also wore an expression of deepest melancholy, and Annabelle was careful to hide a slightly ironic though sympathetic smile. She recognised the symptoms. Her mother was indulging herself yet again by another spell of mourning her lost youth.

'Good morning, Mama,' the girl spoke cheerfully. 'What would you like to do today? Would you care to go out for a drive later on?'

Solange draped herself on the couch, uttering a doleful sigh.

'I suppose that we might, but where? What is there to see? Whom could we call upon?'

'We have been home for more than three weeks now. Do you not think it is time we began renewing old acquaintances?'

'With whom, pray?' A trace of acerbity banished the dismalness of tone. 'As you say, Annabelle, we have been here over three weeks, but no one other than Mr Lockwood has been near us.'

'Perhaps people do not yet know that we are back in England.'

'Not know? Of course they must, by now. Lockwood knew, so you may depend on it that word has gone round.' Solange heaved another sigh. 'No, my poor daughter, there can be little doubt that we have been wholly cast out by Society. The scandal of four years ago is still hanging over us. I am forced to conclude that from now on we shall not receive a single invitation. Even the Palmer-Austins, who were our best friends and nearest neighbours, have not sent a word to welcome us back.'

Annabelle bit her lip.

'You know very well, Mama, that the day after our arrival Proudy told us that the Palmer-Austins had sold the Grange and gone to live in Italy for Mrs Palmer-Austin's health's sake. A new owner now occupies their house; a widower named Mr Francis Trecarey. From Cornwall, I understand.'

'A heathen area of the country!' Solange shuddered delicately. 'And has *he* made any attempt to call on us, his next neighbours? No, he has not.'

'Perhaps he has not liked to foist himself upon us if he is a gentleman of sensitive feeling,' Annabelle suggested reasonably.

Solange appeared to consider this. 'I still think he might have sent his card round.'

'Perhaps he feels the first move should come from us.' With sudden decision, Annabelle jumped up and went to sit at the escritoire.

'To whom are you writing, child?' Solange asked in a languid voice.

'A note to Mr Trecarey, asking if he might care to come and take a glass of Madeira with us before luncheon.'

Solange sat upright abruptly.

'Annabelle, you are not! I forbid it!'

'Why ever should you, Mama?'

'Because—because this Mr Trecarey from Cornwall is probably a wild man. All the Cornish are wild, uncouth people, quite uncivilised and unsuitable to cultivate as friends.'

'Mama, what prejudiced nonsense you do talk upon occasions,' Annabelle said mildly. 'The Cornish gentry are every bit as "civilised" as we are here.'

'He may think it forward of you to suggest it.'

'He is far more likely to think it an act of neighbourly courtesy.'

Annabelle deftly folded and sealed her missive and pulled the bell-rope. When a footman appeared, she requested him to take the letter round to Winkworth Grange at once and await an answer. While waiting, they talked of other matters. Solange complained of what she termed Suzanne's 'impertinence' the previous evening.

'Please try to bear with her, Mama. She is very unhappy now that she thinks Gilbert Distel has deserted her, and you know how attached she is to me.'

'She could scarcely have hoped he would actually marry her! She has no dowry, nothing.'

'Monsieur Distel had expressed a hope of making her his wife when he was in a position to do so,' Annabelle said quietly. 'She loves him.'

Solange gave a small unsympathetic sniff.

'I wonder where he went off to that night, and what has become of him?'

'Probably we shall never find out,' Annabelle responded with a sigh.

'And how shall we ever learn of my poor brother's

fate?' Solange mourned. 'Oh, I am not at all in the mood for entertaining! I shall return to my room.'

'No, Mama, please,' Annabelle begged. 'I am sure some fresh company would do you good. If Mr Trecarey comes and we do not like him, we need not continue the acquaintance.'

'Oh, very well, since it means so much to you,' Solange said pettishly. A few minutes later, however, when the footman returned bearing a letter expressing Mr Francis Trecarey's pleased acceptance of their invitation, she was on her feet in a trice.

'Annabelle, summon Suzanne at once. She must arrange my hair. What shall I wear? That coffee morning gown trimmed with ruched satin ribbon? Or do you consider it is too sober in effect? One does not wish to seem *dull*, even to a stranger. Perhaps my new hyacinth blue with the cream lace fichu? Blue always suits both you and me because of the colour of our eyes, and I think that blue gown makes me look younger. What do you prefer?'

'Suzanne shall go with you to your room at once and help you decide. Mr Trecarey sounds a pleasant gentleman. We must hope to impress him as likeable neighbours.'

'Oh, la la! it is his task to impress us,' Solange declared, but she hastened from the room to make her preparations.

Annabelle was pleased to observe such signs of animation in her mother. If Mr Trecarey did indeed prove to be a pleasant new acquaintance, he might at least provide the means of renewed entry into local society for Solange. New interests and new friends were precisely what Mama needed now, she thought.

Half an hour before luncheon, when he was announced, the first impression created was certainly agreeable. Mr Trecarey proved to be a stockily built man, of late middle age and silver-haired, but his ruddiness of complexion tokened much time spent in healthy outdoor occupations. His skin was weather-beaten, not empurpled by alcohol as was so often the case with gentlemen of his standing. His manners were correct, if a trifle bluff.

'My lady, great pleasure, great pleasure to meet you and your charming daughter. Considered several times calling on you, but did not wish to intrude.'

'There, Mama, did I not declare it must be Mr Trecarey's natural sensitivity that was preventing him from making our acquaintance?' Annabelle said in a forthright tone. 'We are delighted to meet you, sir.'

Solange unfurled her fan and looked at him over the top of it. Suzanne's rapid ministrations had produced a charming result. A small lace cap was perched on Milady's dove-grey curls, and the blue of her gown matched the eyes considering him over the fan. Annabelle could see Solange was trying to make up her mind whether to treat him with French aristocratic hauteur, or with the graciousness expected of an English country lady. The latter choice won the day.

'Sir, you must forgive our tardiness in inviting you here. We have been so much distressed ...' Solange launched into the shocking tale of the Comte's arrest and their flight from Camoret. Mr Trecarey appeared suitably horrified.

'My daughter is now true mistress of Sarne,' Solange concluded, looking pathetically wistful. 'I have no heart for anything. I am retired from the world.'

'My dear lady, I trust not. Tut, but what a shocking tale you have to tell! You have had some harrowing experiences, but even though you may have chosen to eschew London life, trust you may still honour our local Assemblies?' Trecarey exclaimed.

Solange shrugged sadly.

'Come, come,' persisted the gentleman. 'If I may remark on it, you are far too young and good-looking to stay hidden within the walls of Sarne. I had hoped ... if you would not consider it too presumptuous ...'

'What, pray, Mr Trecarey?'

'Well, since coming here, I have received many kind invitations from our neighbours in the County. Want to return the kindnesses, y'know, but hardly know how to set about it without a hostess. M' wife, you know. Quite lost without the poor soul. Was wondering, Ma'am, if I might prevail on you, as my nearest neighbour, to act hostess for me?'

Solange looked taken aback and was opening her mouth to state, with some renewal of hauteur, that on such brief acquaintance he *was* being too presumptuous, when Annabelle clapped her hands.

'Why, Mama, what a perfectly splendid notion! That way you will be certain to meet everyone again. All your old friends, and new ones too, I dare say.'

'But, Annabelle, I have not taken part in any functions since your poor Papa ...'

'Papa died four years ago. I know he would not have wished you to continue pining. Mr Trecarey, it is kind of you to suggest such a thing! I am sure my mother will be charmed to accept.'

'Will you, Lady Solange? 'Twould be a great service. I'd thought of giving a dinner party at the Grange. Thanks to all, y' know, who've treated me with generous hospitality. I'd be much honoured, Ma'am, if you'd agree to assist me.'

'Well, sir,' Solange murmured, 'since you put it like that, how can I refuse?'

'Capital! Capital!' Mr Trecarey's rosy face beamed. 'Shall we fix on a date at once and begin making our plans?'

Annabelle, pleased and amused, left them talking and wandered out into the garden. The previous night's storm had soaked everything and flowers were still hanging heads heavy with drenched petals. Should she walk down now to the priest's cottage and question him concerning both André and Major Lockwood? No, it must wait until later. It would seem discourteous to absent herself from the drawing-room for too long. She wondered what André was doing now. Had he already returned to French soil? Oh, if she only had some idea of his mysterious mission!

As she seated herself on a rustic bench, the sound of carriage wheels approaching along the drive caused her to glance over her shoulder. A closed carriage was rattling its way over the gravel; a carriage piled with trunks and boxes, two pack-horses tied behind, bearing still more luggage.

Her heart gave a startled leap and she stood up quickly, watching as it came to rest before the front steps. Even as a footman came hurrying down to open the door and stand aside, allowing the occupant to alight, she guessed who must have arrived.

From the coach, elegant in midnight blue with ruffles of snowy lace at wrists and throat, issued the tall, arrogant figure of Gaspard, Marquis d'Hubert.

CHAPTER
FIVE

ANNABELLE had time to retreat hastily indoors via the french window, only to find the drawing-room empty. Glancing out, she observed the backs of Mr Trecarey and her mother disappearing along one of the yew walks. They were still deep in earnest conversation. Annabelle seated herself and snatched up the firescreen she had begun to embroider. When the Marquis was announced, she presented a picture of innocent occupation.

Gaspard came in, placed a hand upon his heart and made an elegant leg.

'Mademoiselle Annabelle, my fairest one,' in exquisite French, 'what inestimable pleasure it gives my travel-wearied eyes to gaze at last upon your face and form.'

A month ago, she would have been entranced had he made her such a flattering speech. Having totally fallen out of love with him and into love with a particular dream, she now only experienced a most unladylike desire to burst out laughing. She managed to control it, rose, and made him a deep curtsey.

'I trust your journey has not been too exhausting, sir? Albert, a glass of wine for Monsieur le Marquis, then you may leave us.'

As the footman poured the wine, Gaspard sank upon the couch, produced a wisp of lace from his bosom, and delicately patted his lips.

'Unutterably wearisome,' he murmured wanly. 'I

was forced to stop at a wayside hostelry to change my horses. A disgusting place; cheap wine, the meanest food cooked quite appallingly, and all managed by a dog of an innkeeper without respect for his betters. I was obliged to teach him a lesson in manners, and left the mark of my cane across his grimy cheek.'

'Oh dear,' said the girl, but the moment the door closed behind the departing footman, she leaned forward eagerly, hands clasped.

'Gaspard, I must enquire immediately, have you any news of my uncle the Comte? Has he been released and permitted to return home?'

An expression of suitable sorrow replaced the Marquis's world-weary air.

'Alas, *ma chère*, my news can only serve to distress you. I have not been to Paris myself. It scarcely seemed wise under the circumstances. But the news-sheets are full of it. Also, Monsieur le Comte's lawyer paid me a personal visit but four days since.'

'Tell me at once,' Annabelle begged, feeling herself growing pale. 'Spare me nothing.'

'It seems my poor godfather was most roughly used by the *canaille*, taken before a People's Court and condemned out of hand.'

'*Condemned?*' She was horror-stricken.

'To death. For treason against the State by aiding in their Majesties' plot to escape justice, so 'tis said.'

'He is to die?' Annabelle whispered.

Even as she spoke, in the midst of her distress, she noticed something. The Marquis had lost his pose of complete exhaustion and was leaning forward watching her. His bluish-grey eyes, normally so bored, held a curiously calculating expression, as if he were measuring the sincerity of her anguish.

'My dear Annabelle,' he murmured, 'you need not quite despair as yet. The Comte's lawyer, apparently, put forward a heart-rending plea for mercy, and it was partially granted. Sentence was finally deferred for one month while consultations take place. It is possible that Camoret may be reprieved, and his sentence commuted to imprisonment for life.'

It was almost as terrible; perhaps more so for a man of the Comte's station in life. To spend the rest of his days shut up with thieves and murderers, the very lowest of the low! Annabelle shuddered. It was impossible to contemplate. Death, to be undertaken with courageous dignity, must surely seem infinitely preferable to such a man as the Comte de Camoret. She was speechless with shock and horror, only vaguely aware of Gaspard's cold eyes watching her.

He leaned back and flicked a speck from the sleeve of his coat.

'Where is my godmother, Lady Solange? I trust she is well?'

'She is out in the garden, walking with a neighbour of ours, a Mr Trecarey,' Annabelle answered mechanically. Mama! she thought. This appalling news would half kill her.

The veil of bored indifference settled again over Gaspard's face.

'I am distressed to be the bearer of such sad tidings.' His voice was entirely without real sympathetic warmth, Annabelle realised. 'However,' he went on, 'there is nothing we can do. As I say, his lawyer called on me a few days ago with certain information. It seems the Comte holds out small chance for his own survival. He has made over the Camoret estate to you.'

Annabelle uttered a small gasp. Watching her, the

Marquis continued:

'Alas, there is still quite a probability that the château may be confiscated by those now temporarily in power. We must hope that does not happen. I deem the wisest plan must be for us to announce our betrothal at once, and arrange for our nuptial Mass. We will return to France and live at Camoret as soon as we may.'

This stark announcement had the effect of bringing Annabelle out of her state of shock. She stared at the Marquis, noting the manner in which he was still observing her. A wave of revulsion swept through her. She had thought him so splendid, the epitome of haughty elegance and noble grace. Now she perceived that his mouth was sensual, but also thin-lipped and rather cruel. His handsome face, with its aquiline features powdered and patched in the height of fashion, seemed like an arrogant mask, the eyes hard as agate.

Surprisingly, another face rose in her mind's eye, a face that was not handsome but possessed an oddly rugged attraction with its humorous mouth and golden hazel eyes. She might detest the name of Lockwood to the depth of her being, but at least the Major owned the strong features of a man, not a 'painted popinjay', as he had dubbed the Marquis d'Hubert.

For a moment, in a strange kind of hallucination, she equated the strong and humorous countenance of Major Marcus Lockwood with her private knowledge of André, her mysterious beloved. Somehow that face seemed to fit the personality of the French Captain.

The sudden thought shocked and angered her and she dismissed it. At least, she thought wryly, she could now see the Marquis d'Hubert in a wholly different

light to the one that had dominated her schoolgirl
daydreams.

She drew herself upright.

'Sir, I am sensible of the honour you do me in
wishing to make me your wife, and I am aware that it
was also my uncle's wish, but I regret having to remind
you that circumstances have altered. In brief, I cannot
possibly marry you.'

The expression of ludicrous astonishment that shot
across his face almost made her laugh again, albeit a
trifle hysterically. The Marquis also sat upright with
alacrity.

'Mademoiselle, what is this you are saying? You
cannot be my wife? But it is arranged. The Comte . . .'

'Sorrowfully, the Comte is no longer in a position to
control my future. By the terms of my father's will, I
am now my own mistress, and mistress of this manor.
Also, as you know, I stand to inherit a fortune from
my paternal grandmother; but only, I am obliged to
tell you, if I wed a gentleman of English blood.'

'Marry an Englishman!' he gasped, shaken out of
his customary pose of world-weary indifference to
everything happening around him. '*C'est impossible!*
Camoret could not have known of this.'

'He did not. My mother was afraid to tell him. I
knew nothing of it either until recently.'

Gaspard exclaimed: 'I think—I believe—I have a
right to know how much you are to inherit?'

'Forty thousand pounds,' Annabelle told him
bluntly, and saw him give a thin-lipped smile, obvious
relief replacing the angry shock in his eyes. He leaned
back.

'A tolerable amount, I grant you, but we shall
scarcely need it. I am happy to tell you that I have
managed to arrange for most of my assets to be taken

out of France until such time as we may return to normal living circumstances there. We need lack for nothing, Annabelle. Forget your grandmother's pittance. We can do without it.'

'The money is not of primary importance to me. My home most certainly is.'

His eyes narrowed.

'Your home? Sarne Manor? I do not understand you.'

Annabelle sighed. 'Reluctantly, I see I must disclose the facts. If I do not, Mama will certainly do so at the first opportunity. The Comte de Camoret does not know this, but before my father died he came to—an honourable agreement with a certain Sir Julian Lockwood; namely, that when I became eighteen, I should marry Lockwood's son, Marcus. If I fail in this, Major Lockwood may claim Sarne and its contents from me.'

'Lockwood? Lockwood?' The Marquis almost spluttered. 'Surely that is the fellow who ...'

'Who fought a duel with my father in which they both suffered fatal wounds.'

'*Mon Dieu!*' gasped the Marquis.

'It surprises you, no doubt. The fact remains. This arrangement must take precedence over any agreement my uncle may have made with you.'

'Takes precedence?' Momentarily, Gaspard looked upon the verge of having an apoplectic fit. His eyes actually bulged, and two bright patches showed through the powder on his cheekbones. His upper lip drew back almost in a snarl as he leapt to his feet.

Annabelle stood up too, somewhat apprehensively. She had never seen him look so furious. With a visible effort, he regained control of himself.

'Mademoiselle,' he said with intense hauteur, 'I am

appalled by what you tell me. That some whipper-snapper of an English army officer should dare to try and *take precedence* over myself, a member of one of France's most noble families! Tell me immediately where this—this person may be found, so that I may defend my honour without a moment's delay.'

'Oh sir, I do implore you, no bloodshed!'

'Bloodshed!' snarled the Marquis. 'I shall take the most exquisite pleasure in drawing forth every drop of blood from his anaemic veins. Or if he insists upon pistols, send a bullet straight to his impudent heart. I command you to inform me at once where I may discover this jackanapes, so that I may send my seconds.'

'Oh, Gaspard, please contain your wrath,' Annabelle besought in genuine alarm. 'I—I believe Major Lockwood may well prove an expert swordsman, and—and in any case, duelling is now much frowned upon in England. If either of you killed, or even severely wounded the other, you would be forced to quit this land at once. And I have no wish to be the cause of any violence.'

'Rest tranquil, you could in no way be held responsible. This is a matter of honour which must be settled between Lockwood and myself. Ladies,' pronounced the Marquis in sweepingly crushing tones, 'cannot be expected to appreciate the delicacy of such a situation, but it is entirely necessary, I assure you. Where is this creature?'

'I do not know. Truly I do not, though I believe he lives in London,' Annabelle said reluctantly.

'Ah. Then I shall leave at once and seek him out to settle the affair forthwith.'

'But what of the consequences?'

'Any consequences shall be dealt with, do not fear,'

he told her grandly. 'If need be, we can leave England for a time. Perhaps go to Switzerland. We can be married there as well as here.'

'No, we can *not!*' Annabelle stamped her foot in sudden rage. 'Allow me to remind you, Gaspard, that I have already refused to marry you.'

The Marquis looked slightly startled, then spoke soothingly as one might to a fractious child.

'Come, come, *ma fille*, you cannot persuade me that you would actually prefer to wed this English fellow—someone without either wealth or noble blood?'

'Major Lockwood *is* of good family,' she retorted defiantly.

'An adventurer, no less,' Gaspard continued, ignoring the interruption. 'You'd marry such a person merely to retain Sarne Manor? I cannot think you would really be so foolish. Listen. We have no need of anything you may own here, especially if we have Camoret in addition to my own estates. It can only be a short while, a few months perhaps, before matters resolve themselves in France and order is restored there.'

'In *your* country, sir. England is *my* true country and Sarne my home. No, I have no desire to marry Major Lockwood, although I still have to discover a means to avoid doing so and still keep my lands.'

The Marquis gave a short laugh and his lip curled.

'Your solution is obvious. I shall deal with your troublesome English Major by killing him, then Sarne will remain yours. *Ours!* We can live abroad for a while until the scandal blows over, then divide our time between here and France as we choose.'

Annabelle regarded him steadily.

'Tell me, Gaspard, why are you so set upon marry-

ing me? I am sure you do not love me. Am I to assume
it is merely to win Camoret into your own possession?'

His eyes flickered, his look falling away from hers.

'The Comte desires our marriage. Perhaps he has a
particular reason.'

'What reason?'

He shrugged, but she had the feeling he was holding
something back. His gaze roved over her, from her
soft fair curls down over her bare neck and shoulders,
lingering on the curve of her small breasts, then he
said coldly:

'Love is for sentimental fools, but I am happy with
such a choice of bride. You are very beautiful,
Annabelle. The noblest blood flows in your veins even
though you are, unfortunately, part English. But you
will make a perfect ornament for my house.'

'*Your* house?' she flashed. 'Camoret is mine, and I
tell you here and now, Gaspard d'Hubert, that
nothing in heaven or earth will ever force me into
wedlock with you, for I have realised at last what you
are. Greedy, over-ambitious, arrogant, and wholly
indifferent to the fate of my poor uncle, whatever you
may pretend! He, alas, was too blind to observe that
for himself. Kindly leave Sarne at once. I never wish to
see you again.'

For a terrible moment, she thought he might strike
her. His face turned livid, and such a look of malevo-
lent fury came into his eyes that she actually blenched
as he took a step towards her.

'So,' he hissed between clenched teeth, 'that is what
you think of me, is it? Well, let me tell you, Annabelle
Sarne, *I* have decided upon our future. I shall leave
you now to go and seek for Lockwood. Once I have
put him out of my way, I shall return.'

He lunged suddenly, grasped her wrist and jerked

...er against him. 'Yes, I shall return.' His face came
close to hers so that she smelt the stale perfume
enshrouding him. 'I shall claim you to wife and take
much delight in bringing you to heel; break that bold
unwomanly spirit you possess. 'Twill make my
revenge that much sweeter.'

Swiftly, he bent his head and planted a fierce kiss on
her mouth, almost biting at her lips, then flung her
away scornfully. She fell against the chair on which
she had been sitting.

'*Au revoir*, Mademoiselle Arrogance, Lady of
Sarne,' he sneered. 'I can have little patience with
rebellious females, women or bitches.' And turning,
he swung out of the room.

Annabelle pulled herself slowly up on to the chair
and sat rubbing her bruised lips with the back of her
hand. Revenge? What on earth could he mean?
Revenge against whom?

She was shaking with revulsion, shock and fright,
but a hot flame of rage, searing up inside her,
quenched other emotions. Aristocrat? He was no
more than a coarse bully, a lout. She would give orders
never to let him be admitted again. But oh, what
would happen now? He had gone to seek Lockwood
and challenge him. If they met, how could bloodshed
possibly be avoided?

She did not think the Major was the kind of man to
turn the other cheek. The death of one or the other
might well be laid at her door. She shivered at the
mere idea. Yet no one could actually hold her to
blame. *She* was a victim of circumstances.

There seemed no way in which she could warn
Lockwood of the Marquis being out for his blood. If it
did come to swordplay, whom would she prefer to be
the victor? Despite all, a voice in the back of her mind

whispered that she hoped it would be Lockwood who
survived. She could not imagine, now, how she had
ever thought d'Hubert attractive. Determined as she
was to prevent Lockwood from taking Sarne, she
could not bring herself to hope his death in duelling
might solve her problems for her.

From the window she watched the Marquis's laden
carriage and packhorses disappearing along the
driveway, then she saw her mother hurrying across the
lawn. Solange entered by the french door in quite
unladylike haste and exclaimed immediately: 'Whose
carriage was that I just saw leaving? Whom have I
missed, *chèrie*?'

'Well, Mama, actually it was Gaspard, newly come
from France.'

'Gaspard!' Then Solange clasped ecstatic hands.
'My dearest daughter, you have seen reason at last
and sent him away! You have perceived the wisdom of
choosing to wed Major Lockwood after all.'

'No, I have not,' snapped Annabelle, tried beyond
endurance. 'Do not leap to conclusions, Mama. But
certainly I dismissed the Marquis. He behaved in a
most uncouth and discourteous manner. I have been
mistaken in my view of him. I freely admit that now.'

'Why? What did he do?' Solange looked
astonished.

Annabelle told her.

'He—he misused you, *threatened* you?' gasped her
mother. 'He forced his attentions on you and kissed
you by force?'

'He did indeed. Perceive the marks on my wrist
where he grasped hold of it.'

Annabelle held out her arm for inspection. Solange
peered, gasped, and sinking on the couch, began to
fan herself.

'Well, I am appalled! I should never have believed that Gaspard would behave so shockingly. At least we must now be agreed that he is not the proper husband for you?'

'We are certainly agreed on that. He said the strangest thing; that to "break my spirit", as he termed it, would "make his revenge all the sweeter".'

Solange looked blank.

'Revenge? What did he mean?'

'I cannot imagine. I thought you might be able to enlighten me.'

'Me? How could I?' After a pause, Solange shrugged. 'A strange remark to make, indeed! And you say he has gone in search of Major Lockwood and means to call him out? Merciful heaven, what will happen? They may kill each other, as Michael and Julian did. Oh, I simply cannot endure all that over again,' she wailed, her chins beginning to quiver. 'Is there no end to our dreadful anxieties?'

'I'm afraid not as yet, Mama. Gaspard brought news of—of my uncle.'

'Of Henri? What news? Tell me quickly.'

'He is—to remain in prison for the moment,' Annabelle said carefully.

'Ah, *mon pauvre frère*,' Solange wept. 'What will become of him? Had Gaspard seen him?'

'No. He did not think it politic to visit Paris at this time. He intends remaining in England now for some while, but *I* shall not give him house-room at Sarne.'

'I should think not indeed!' exclaimed Solange, successfully distracted from the Comte's fate at least for the moment. 'I am most deeply shocked to think he could treat you with so little respect. He is supposed to be a gentleman and from one of France's most noble families.'

'Aristocratic blood does not necessarily make him a gentleman in the truest sense of the word, Mama. Mr Trecarey, on the other hand, does seem both charming and agreeable,' Annabelle added, in a further attempt to distract her mother from dangerous topics.

Tears forgotten, Solange beamed.

'A *most* charming man, and eager to pursue an acquaintance with us. I am delighted now at the prospect of acting hostess to his guests. We have begun making our plans. Rather than a small dinner-party, I suggested we might hold a soirée and invite everyone of consequence in the County. He appeared wholly enchanted by the idea.'

'I am glad, Mama. It will give you an interest to plan for it.'

'Yes.' Solange shot her a slightly shamed look. 'It is tragic indeed about poor Henri, but there is nothing we can do, is there? Nor can we do anything about the Marquis and Mr Lockwood, so there can be no point in repining.'

'It is sensible of you to take that view,' Annabelle agreed quietly.

Nothing could ease her own intense anxiety as to the future, but it would provide considerable relief if Mama developed a more cheerful attitude, she thought. On this occasion she was glad that Solange's somewhat shallow nature could find distraction more readily than some others might have been able to do.

Later that afternoon, Annabelle went to Father Martin's cottage again. She found the old man pottering in his vegetable patch, gathering herbs for a stew.

'Good day, my daughter. You wished to speak with me?'

'Somewhere where we cannot be overheard, Father,' she replied, rising from her curtsey.

'Then come into my house. I am entirely alone.'

She followed him inside then, characteristically, came straight to the point.

'Father, last evening when I called to see you, I could not help observing two half-empty glasses of wine on the table. I formed a conclusion that your visitor was still in the house—but wished not to be seen.'

The priest sat down, folded his hands, and regarded her with wholly unruffled serenity. 'Did you, my child?'

'Yes. I—I do not want to pry into things that are not my concern, but—but I have a special reason for desiring to know who was here last night.'

'Would you care to tell me that reason?'

Annabelle explained her problem in regard to the Marquis d'Hubert and Major Lockwood, mentioning Lockwood's visit. She also told him of her meeting with the French captain in the wood near Calais, but not the encounter of the previous night, although she knew in her heart that she ought to make confession. When her voice finally faltered into silence, Martin sat looking at her thoughtfully before speaking.

'My dear child, I see your difficulty. At present, I can only counsel patience. Wait upon events; problems often solve themselves. With regard to Monsieur le Marquis, I think you are well rid of him. His behaviour towards you has certainly not been that of a gentleman, so let us hope he does not come back to trouble you further. As for Major Lockwood...' He paused.

'You do know the Major? My steward tells me he has been here before,' Annabelle said, watching him.

'I am acquainted with him. He came to see me in my capacity as a priest, to seek information regarding our Faith.'

'Oh!' Annabelle felt surprised. 'But—it was not he who was here last night?'

Father Martin smiled. She thought it a remarkably bland smile.

'Someone called to see me on a matter of religious belief. It need not concern you, my dear.'

'I see.'

There really seemed nothing more to say. Evidently Father Martin had no intention of satisfying her curiosity about his secret nocturnal guest. Uncomfortably, she rose to leave, wishing she had not ventured upon the subject. She found she could not voice, after all, a sudden extraordinary suspicion that had taken root in her mind.

CHAPTER
SIX

As soon as darkness fell, the Comte de Camoret wrapped his cloak around him for extra warmth and lay down on the pallet in one corner of his cell.

In the past six weeks, since his arrest, a terrible change had come over the head of the House of Camoret. He had lost weight, and not only because of poor prison food; his lawyer had brought him funds with which to bribe the gaolers for some improvements in his living conditions. Fear, suspicion and despair had wrought the drastic alteration. If he had possessed a looking-glass, he would hardly have recognised the pallid, haggard man whose flesh now hung loosely on his bones, and whose hair had turned nearly white in less than two months.

At least he now owned privacy, although in the past few hours he had begun to wonder if that were so much to be desired, since it meant he had nothing to distract him from himself. Until this morning he had shared the cell with two other men. Today, one had gone to a different part of France to begin a long sentence for robbery with violence. The other had taken leave of the Comte with enviable controlled dignity and set forth upon that journey from which no traveller ever returns. By now his headless body, covered by quicklime, would be lying buried somewhere within the prison graveyard. His crime had been similar to that ascribed to the Comte; treason

against the People. He had aided a famous French
politician, who favoured the *ancien règime*, to leave
the country against orders.

The Comte de Camoret possessed one crumb of
comfort. His lawyer had been able to reassure him
that his sister, the Lady Solange, and his dear niece
Annabelle were safely out of France and back at
Sarne. The lawyer had received an anonymous message stating that fact.

The hearing of the Comte's case had been a farce.
With the public seats packed with the *canaille*, all
screeching and constantly interrupting proceedings
with catcalls, his counsel had been able to say little.
The Prosecution had brought in witness after witness,
total strangers to the Comte, with evidence to say he
had participated in the Royal plot to leave the city.
The Comte was no fool, and well aware of the
jealousies and strivings for power in Court circles.
Since he was wholly innocent of the charge, there
could be little doubt that someone had plotted his
downfall. It might have been anyone anxious to
ingratiate themselves with the newly-powerful Citizens' Committee. Yet among the unknown 'witnesses' speaking against him, there had been one
vaguely familiar face. After a while, the Comte had
managed to identify it. The man was his godson Gaspard's head footman.

The fellow swore he had 'overheard conversations
with persons unknown', incriminating the Comte de
Camoret. In the end, his counsel had been reduced to
putting up a passionate plea for mercy, and execution
of sentence had been deferred. But the Comte enter-
tained small hope of permanent reprieve. And after
all, might it not be preferable to go forth and meet his
end with dignity as his cell companion had done that

ery morning? That would be better by far than rot-
ing forgotten in some awful prison hole.

Why should his godson, whom he had always
reated with such special consideration, wish to betray
him, perhaps see him dead?

There might be a reason, a deeply personal reason,
but how could Gaspard have learned *that* secret?
Unless Marguerite herself had told him?

As he tried, vainly, to compose himself for sleep,
he Comte became aware of a commotion outside his
cell door; voices, footsteps clattering on the stone
floor, a sharp command. He half-rose as the door was
flung open and lantern light shone in his eyes. What
now? Despite his resolve to show nothing other than
dignified courage on all occasions, his heart thudded
anxiously.

'Citizen Camoret, get up at once. Clothe yourself.'

Beyond the open door in the passage, he could see
uniforms.

'What is happening? What do you want?' he asked,
getting up stiffly.

'Obey!' growled the gaoler. 'An order has come
through for your transfer.'

'Transfer? Where? By whose command? Where
are you taking me?' the Comte demanded with as
much hauteur as he could muster, scrambling his few
possessions together.

'Not my business. The papers are in order.'

'May I be permitted to see them?'

The officer in charge of the escort, a captain, stepped forward and held them out. As he did so, he stared
unblinkingly at the Comte. He was a well-set-up, tall
fellow, and as his face moved out of the shadow the
Comte particularly noticed his eyes; striking in colour,
long-lashed and strangely beautiful in a man. The

paper, authorising the Comte's removal to another
prison in a different part of Paris, appeared correctly
signed.

'Come along, come along, I've not got all night,' the
gaoler grumbled.

As the Comte stepped outside the cell, soldiers took
up position on either side of him and the captain
moved behind. A few moments later they were out in
the prison yard and he could feel the cooling night air
on his cheek. He was hurried into a waiting coach, its
window blinds down. The captain climbed in with
him, and the escort rode on either side, close to the
doors.

They travelled without speech; each man, for
reasons of his own, preferring the detachment of
silence. Camoret was wondering what this change
could portend. Was he being transferred to begin a
long-term sentence, or—or was this new prison to be,
ultimately, the place of his execution?

When the carriage finally slowed to a halt, he was
preparing to receive the order to alight when the
captain suddenly astonished him by leaning over and
grasping his wrist, at the same time making a signal for
quiet. Bewildered, the Comte got stiffly out into the
roadway—and stood amazed. This was no prison
yard. They were in a mean street, but one that was
oddly familiar. At its end he recognised the towering
steep of Montmartre hill. A second later, he was being
hustled unceremoniously through a narrow doorway
and up some twisty stairs into a low-ceilinged room. A
figure, dimly to be seen by the light from one smoky
candle, rose from behind a table and bowed.

'Monsieur le Comte, you have made the journey
safely!'

The Comte uttered a gasp.

'Distel! Holy Mother of God, it is Distel!'

'Your servant, Monsieur. Please be seated.' The erstwhile secretary indicated a chair. They had been left alone in the room. 'May I ask how you find yourself? Are you in reasonable health, sir?'

'I—I am well enough. Distel, what are you doing here? What is this place? Why have I been brought here?' the Comte exclaimed.

'It will be my pleasure to explain in just one moment.'

Swiftly and quietly, Distel crossed the room and jerked open the door. He nodded with satisfaction and, closing it again came to stand opposite the Comte.

'Monsieur, in a single phrase, you have been rescued. Tomorrow, if fortune continues to smile on us, we shall leave Paris, travel to England, and you will be reunited with Lady Solange and Mademoiselle Sarne.'

'Free?' muttered the Comte. 'Am I dreaming?'

'It is no dream, I assure you. Tonight we hoodwinked the guards and effected your release from prison.'

'Ah, *mon Dieu*,' gasped Camoret. 'It is true! You have rescued me! Distel, my loyal, faithful fellow, how can I ever thank you?'

'Thanks are not due to me. It was not I who took the major risks.'

'Not you...? Then ... ah, it was the officer in charge! He was not genuine? A disguise?'

'A disguise, sir, indeed, and the soldiers were his men; the papers were forgeries.'

'Holy Virgin, that is fantastic!' cried the Comte. 'Where is he? I must thank him without delay, for saving probably my life, certainly my sanity. The

young captain, with those quite remarkable eyes!
Where is he?'

'He has gone, Monsieur. André never waits for
thanks.'

'André?'

'It is the name by which he is known, the only name,
and he would not be happy if he heard your comment
on his looks. He regards those somewhat exceptional
eyes of his as a serious drawback. For a man who
wishes to retain anonymity, they are too easily recalled.'

'So I can well understand. My good Distel; explain
all, I beg you. My head is reeling. Who is this captain
who risks his life for such as myself? What is your own
relationship to him? What drama is being enacted
here? I implore you to tell me.'

'It might be—safer for you to know as little as
possible. We are not yet safely out of Paris. I will tell
you this much. There is a group of men, some French,
some English, who are concerned about the trend of
events in France. We have sworn to succour those
wrongfully accused of "crimes against the People".
André is our leader; I, his second in command. That is
all I may tell you, for we are all bound by solemn oaths
of secrecy.'

'Well . . .' murmured the Comte, astounded. 'Well,
my good Distel. . . . How long has this been going on?
When you were in my employ at Camoret, were you
engaged in this work also?'

'We have helped a number of *emigrés* to leave this
country,' Distel admitted in a cautious tone.

'And now it is my turn. I am entirely in your hands.
What must I do? What news is there? Have you any
news of my château?'

'Camoret is still untouched. It has not been over-

un. The house is closed, the servants dismissed, all
except your steward and his wife, who are loyal to you
and have stayed to care for the place until such time as
it may be deemed safe for you to return there.'

'Thank heaven! Fearing myself doomed, I have
signed papers making the whole estate over to my
niece Annabelle. My lawyer has them.'

'So I understand.'

'Do you, indeed!' The Comte eyed his erstwhile
secretary thoughtfully. 'You seem to know a considerable amount, my dear Distel. Tell me, have you
any information concerning the whereabouts of my
godson, the Marquis d'Hubert?'

Gilbert Distel turned and began pouring out two
measures of wine from a carafe on the table. His face
was hidden from the Comte. 'I believe that he left
France for England some two weeks ago.'

Camoret gave a short sigh.

'Travelling to Sarne, I assume? You knew, of
course, of my plan to betroth my niece to him?'

'Yes, Monsieur.'

Distel handed a glass of wine to the Comte then
leaned against the table's edge, sipping at his own.

'I am not certain that was such a wise notion after
all,' the Comte said, eyeing him.

'Indeed, sir?'

'Someone,' said the Comte slowly, 'has betrayed
me. Someone arranged for false evidence to be
brought against me, plotting my downfall.'

'But you have no shred of proof as to who that
person might be?'

'None.' There was a pause. 'In the courtroom, one
of the witnesses against me seemed familiar. Later, I
recalled where I had seen him. He was my godson's
chief footman.'

'Ah!'

Words left unspoken hung between them in the silence of the dimly lit room. At last the Comte said heavily: 'I trust we may reach Sarne before my niece' wedding can take place.'

'It might be as well, sir.'

'You say we shall leave Paris tomorrow, Distel?'

'That is the plan. I shall disguise you as a lawyer travelling to Rheims to attend an important trial there. I shall accompany you as your "jackal" False papers have been prepared under the names of Monsieur Jaques Bernard, and his assistant Jean Garôt.'

'You *are* coming with me?'

'Yes. Captain André deems it wiser that I should leave France for a time. We have received information that we are becoming known, and the authorities are seeking our identities. Your release is the last Captain André plans to achieve for a while, at least.'

'I see. And may I not ever see him, to offer him my heartfelt thanks?'

'Perhaps, Monsieur, who can say?' Distel said 'Now, may I suggest some food and then sleep? We must rise early. We shall have much to do to accomplish effective disguises for us both before we leave.

By the time Distel had finished with him the following morning, the Comte could not recognise himself He had always considered his secretary a competent fellow, but had never dreamed that Distel owned such hidden talents. Dark clothing, stuffed to provide him with a paunch, a black wig and gold pince-nez were but a part of the Comte's disguise. Distel also padded his cheeks to plump them out, conjured bushy brows by gumming them in place, and drew melancholy lines about his mouth. A much younger man peered back at the Comte from the mirror; a gentleman who was no longer Henri, urbane Comte de Camoret, but a professional man of somewhat gross aspect. Distel, by alchemy of paint-pot and brush, turned himself into a hollow-cheeked, greedy-eyed, middle-aged man with a dissolute air, yet seeming over-anxious to attend upon his master's every whim.

'You have missed your vocation,' said the Comte, amazed. 'You should go upon the stage, Distel. I am persuaded you could earn a fine living.'

The secretary merely shrugged and smiled.

The Comte knew some bad moments when they had to show their papers at the city gates. Were the forgeries sufficiently convincing? He remained leaning back in his corner of the carriage, eyes closed, affecting a bored weariness with the proceedings, and could hardly believe their good fortune when Distel settled back beside him and they moved on. Some time later, at an inn, they changed carriages. At dusk, in a wood not far from the port of Calais, they abandoned the second vehicle, and Distel led the Comte by a woodland path down to a quiet cove. There, rocking on a choppy sea, a small ship rode at anchor.

As they stood waiting for a boat to come and carry them out, Camoret kept glancing nervously over his shoulder. He was seized by a dreadful fear that soldiers might suddenly emerge from the woods and recapture him. After this taste of hope and freedom, the thought of returning to prison seemed wholly unendurable. Soon, he was being assisted into the rowing boat. Approaching the sloop, he could read its name printed on the prow: *The Swift*.

The ship lived up to its name, for with a stiff breeze behind them and sails unfurled, *The Swift* fairly flew towards the English coast. Distel had made the

crossing several times before on business trips to
Sarne; the Comte had never been afloat. He was
pleased to discover himself to be an excellent sailor
and found the short voyage exhilarating. As the
chalky cliffs round Dover became clearer every
moment, he stood with Distel by the rail.

'Monsieur Distel, I have something I wish to say to
you.'

'Yours to command, Monsieur le Comte.'

'When we were at Camoret,' the Comte began,
seeming to choose his words with care, 'perhaps I did
not always behave to you with the courtesy I might
have done. Perhaps, upon occasion, I was harsh.'

'Never harsh, sir. I was your paid servant. It was
your privilege to order me as you chose,' Distel said
quietly.

The Comte raised a hand.

'We of the nobility have perhaps held too much
control in France for too long, and as a result have
become high-handed in our ways. Certainly I believe
now that I did not reward you fairly for all the work
you did. Sadly, I am no longer in a position to make it
up to you. I shall be obliged to live as my niece
Annabelle's guest, but if she can be of service to you in
any way...'

'Monsieur, there is only one thing I want,' the
secretary interrupted him. 'Your permission and
Mademoiselle Annabelle's to wed her maid Suzanne
Dupont if the young woman will so honour me, and
we can find a means whereby we may live.'

'Most certainly employment must be found for you.
I shall speak to my niece on the subject soon after we
arrive.'

Distel grinned. 'Thank you, Monsieur.'

'So you wish to make Mademoiselle Dupont your

wife? She comes of quite good family. 'Twas a pity her parents died young, leaving her without a dowry. Have you reason to hope she will accept you?'

'I did hope. Now I fear I may be met with coldness.'

'Why should you, my good Distel?'

Distel described briefly their meeting with the French captain in the wood near Calais.

'You understand, Monsieur, that Captain André had given strict orders that at no time must he and I be seen together or in any way connected. Should one of us be arrested, then the other might still be free to continue our work. So, I took myself off into the forest without bidding either your niece or Mademoiselle Suzanne goodbye. I fear they may both think that I deserted them in their hour of need. Perhaps I shall not be forgiven.'

The Comte clicked his tongue.

'Unfortunate! But fear not, my friend, I shall plead your case. Together we must aim to bring this affair of the heart to a happy conclusion.'

In the middle of the following afternoon, Annabelle and Suzanne were sitting together in the rose garden. Annabelle had set herself to distract her companion from the melancholy that had engulfed Suzanne since her confessed belief that Distel had deserted her. They were playing a game of cards. Solange had been taken out driving by Mr Francis Trecarey, intent upon completing their plans for the soirée to be held at Winkworth Grange early in September.

Annabelle was pleasantly astonished by the change in her mother since meeting Trecarey. The gentleman called nearly every day on some pretext or other and Solange always welcomed him. She had begun taking an interest in her looks again, ceased gorging herself on sweetmeats, and took as long over her toilettes as in the days when she was eagerly sought after by London society. Annabelle, always tolerantly aware of her mother's basic vanity, was pleased to see it reasserting itself in more healthy ways than the constant self-pity that had swamped Solange for so long. She liked Mr Trecarey herself; she could find no fault with him. Solange had told her that he had been extremely lonely since his wife died and he appeared delighted to have found new companionship himself.

As the card-game ended in victory for Suzanne, both girls heard the sound of carriage wheels and turned to look across the garden, but it was not Mr Trecarey's carriage returning. Annabelle's heart gave a jolt of fright. Could this be the dreaded moment of Gaspard's reappearance? Had he discovered Lockwood? What terrible happening might have taken place?

Then she gave a cry, for descending from the coach was the unmistakable figure of her uncle, the Comte. Behind her, Suzanne uttered a choked gasp. A second man was alighting; tall, slight in build, soberly clad. Annabelle swung to face her.

'Suzanne! It is Distel!'

The French girl was in the grip of obvious agitation, going pink and pale by turns, tears gathering in her eyes.

'It must be all right. Try to compose yourself.' Annabelle whispered urgently. 'Oh, wonderful! My dear uncle is safe!' And catching up her skirts, she began running towards the steps.

CHAPTER
SEVEN

'UNCLE HENRI! My dear uncle, welcome!' Annabelle would have curtsied, but the Comte, overwhelmed by emotion, drew her into an embrace.

'Uncle, you have been released! They have even permitted you to leave France,' the girl cried joyfully. 'Oh, I am so happy you are safe!'

'My dearest niece! Yes, thank the Holy Virgin, I have been saved, but I was not freed. My presence here is due to Monsieur Distel. He, and others with him, achieved my rescue. It is an amazing story I shall tell you.'

Annabelle faced the secretary, but there was definite reserve in her manner as she extended her hand. From the corner of her eye, she saw Suzanne slipping away from the garden towards the rear of the house. Distel observed it too and his anxious smile faded from lips and eyes.

'Monsieur Distel! I cannot pretend that I am not surprised to see you here, but if indeed you are responsible for my uncle's safety then I must thank you with all my heart.'

'Mademoiselle,' Distel bowed over her hand, 'I am aware that you must be puzzled by my behaviour when last we were together. I fear that Mademoiselle Dupont must also be feeling vexed with me? But if you will allow me to explain...?'

'Certainly you shall have a chance to explain,' broke in the Comte a trifle testily. 'But let us go inside first and refresh ourselves. It has been a tedious journey. Naturally, I have brought no luggage with me, Annabelle...'

'All you need will be provided, *mon oncle*. Yes, let us go in. I am proving a bad hostess.'

The girl turned to speak to one of the footmen nearby.

'The Comte de Camoret will occupy the West Wing, as that is already prepared for a guest. Kindly request Mrs Proudfoot to find accommodation for Monsieur Distel, then have refreshments sent into the drawing-room.'

Leaving the travellers in the care of several servants, she went upstairs in search of Suzanne. She tapped on the French girl's bedroom door, and on entering found Suzanne sitting on a chair. The maid rose at once to curtsey, but Annabelle gestured her to be seated again. Suzanne had not been crying, but her eyes were bright with strain.

'Oh, Mademoiselle...?'

'Monsieur Distel declares he has an explanation for us.' Annabelle went straight to the point. 'Did I not say we should not condemn him out of hand?'

'I...I have not condemned him, but I find it hard to forgive that he could leave in such a manner, without a word to reassure me.'

'I know, but let us hear first what he has to say.' Annabelle paused, regarding her maid critically. 'You are looking peaked,' she pronounced. ''Tis small wonder, but we must change that. It will not do to let Monsieur Distel think you have been pining.'

The French girl did not answer.

'Now listen,' Annabelle said in firm tones. 'You are my friend, Suzanne, and I have recently come to a decision. It is not your fault that you were left orphaned and had to be brought up by the nuns, but it is not suitable that you should continue to do menial tasks for me. In future, I wish you to act only as my companion. I shall tell Mrs Proudfoot to engage an abigail for other work, some young girl who wants to train as a ladies' maid, perhaps. Take off that cap and apron, Suzanne, and put on a prettier gown. *I* shall arrange your hair in more fashionable style.'

'Oh, but Mademoiselle . . .' gasped the French girl.

'And that is another thing,' pursued Annabelle. ''Tis likely we shall have to remain in England for quite a while—perhaps years—so you must improve your English. In future we shall converse in that language. Now, let me see what dresses you own.'

With an air of bewilderment, Suzanne got up and opened the door of her dress closet. Annabelle put her fair head on one side and surveyed the contents, then clicked her tongue.

'All much too drab in shade, except that lavender blue one.'

'That is my best gown, Mademoiselle.'

'Take it out and wear it now. And you must call me simply Annabelle in future. English, Suzanne, English.' And she laughed at her friend's expression of dazed wonder.

'I have a very pretty length of yellow sprigged muslin that I do not need,' she went on. 'It will suit your dark colouring admirably. I shall tell the seamstress to make it up for you at once.'

'Mademoiselle ... Annabelle ... You overwhelm me.'

'Well, if you are to marry the Comte's secretary soon you must be suitably clothed,' Annabelle stated.

'Wed him soon? He—has not asked me.'

'Oh but I think that he may before today is over.'

'I shall not marry him, or—or ever speak to him again unless he can explain satisfactorily why he deserted us that night in Calais,' Suzanne exclaimed with sudden spirit.

'We are about to hear his explanation and if it is not good, it may be necessary to treat him with considerable hauteur. It is always easier to be cool and dignified when well dressed. Do you not agree?' Annabelle enquired, taking up a comb and beginning to arrange Suzanne's hair. 'There, you look quite charming. Pinch your cheeks to give them a good colour, and when we go down, carry yourself proudly. I shall make it clear that you are to be given all the respect due to my dearest friend and companion.'

When they entered the drawing-room, they found the Comte and his secretary already seated there, each holding a glass of wine. Both girls curtsied to Annabelle's uncle, and the gentlemen rose and bowed. Suzanne kept her eyelids down. She could not look at Distel.

'Uncle, Mademoiselle Dupont is no longer a servant in this house,' Annabelle said. 'She is my friend. We have been through much together, and from now on I wish her to be treated solely as my friend and companion.'

Camoret inclined his head.

'Mademoiselle Dupont, please be seated. We have much to tell you both. But first, Annabelle, where is my sister? Is she well?'

'Yes, and much happier now. She has gone out for a drive with our near neighbour, Mr Francis Trecarey. He and Mama have quite taken to each other and are fast becoming friends.'

'Indeed?' The Comte raised his brows with a slight air of withdrawal.

'Mr Trecarey moved into Winkworth Grange last year following his wife's death. He is an extremely agreeable gentleman, one of our Cornish gentry. I feel sure you will like him, uncle,' Annabelle finished quietly.

The Comte nodded but made no comment, turning instead to his secretary.

'Well, my dear Distel, I believe you have something to say to my neice and her companion?'

'Thank you, Monsieur le Comte.' Gilbert Distel's sallow face was rather flushed, his eyes anxious behind their spectacles. 'Ladies, I am fully aware that you must be thinking badly of me, but I swear to you that when I left you in that wood, I already knew you to be in safe hands.'

'What can you mean?' Annabelle asked as Suzanne sat silent, her hands twisted together.

'Because,' the Comte broke in, 'Monsieur Distel is a member of a special band of gallants, both French and English, sworn to aid Frenchmen in need. Frenchmen such as myself, wrongly accused and imprisoned. They have, I understand, aided the escape of several noble families.'

Suzanne made a soft sound and for the first time looked directly at her erstwhile lover. Her eyes were beginning to shine.

Annabelle's heart was beating jerkily. 'Monsieur Distel, I repeat, how did you know we were "in safe hands"?'

'Our captain was there to meet you, Mademoiselle.'

'Captain?'

'Captain André. He had given me strictest orders never to be associated with him before others. Then, if either of us were taken, the second might still be unsuspected and able to pursue our work.'

'I see. This—this "Captain André", he trusts you? You work closely together?'

'I am his first lieutenant,' Distel told them simply, 'but even I do not know who he really is. We have all sworn to obey him without question. That is why I left you so abruptly.' He gazed pleadingly at Suzanne.

'This Captain André must be a truly remarkable man,' observed the Comte. 'He actually bluffed his way into the prison where I was being held; he and four of his men, dressed as soldiers of the National Guard. Disguises, perfect disguises! He carried a false order for my transfer to another gaol, but naturally, they took me instead to a house in the Montmartre district where I found Distel awaiting me.'

'Oh, *mon oncle*, pray continue,' breathed Annabelle.

'André had organised our route out of Paris. We were disguised as a lawyer and his assistant travelling to Rheims. The whole matter went smoothly—the plan was perfectly conceived. My only regret is that I have not been able to see this gallant man to thank him personally.'

'But—but you *did* see him?' Annabelle murmured.

'Briefly. We scarcely spoke. He left before I learned the truth and could express my gratitude.'

Annabelle could hardly wait to ask the Comte to describe André's looks, but a certain shyness held her back, and Distel began speaking again.

'Monsieur le Comte, I fear I have something more to disclose which may well distress and anger you, and perhaps cause anguish to your niece.'

'To Annabelle? Why? What is this?'

Distel looked embarrassed.

'Mademoiselle, I must first ask you if the Marquis d'Hubert has been here recently?'

'Yes, he has. He arrived from France one afternoon about two weeks ago.'

'Ah.' Distel looked even more unhappy. 'Forgive my asking, but I know that your uncle had arranged for your betrothal. Is—are the nuptial plans far advanced?'

Annabelle raised her brows.

'No, sir, they are not. Nor are they likely to be.' She turned to the Comte. 'Uncle, I have no desire to go against your wishes. I dislike excessively having to displease you, but things have changed since last we were together. Under no circumstances will I ever agree to marrying d'Hubert.'

'Thank heaven!' exclaimed the Comte.

They all stared at him, startled.

'You—you no longer wish me to marry Gaspard?'

'No, my dear, I scarcely think I do. But before I give my reason, let us hear what Distel has to tell us.'

The secretary was looking decidedly relieved.

'I have hesitated to speak of this because I have no proof. Doubtless, if taxed, the Marquis would deny it, but the truth is that a few days before your arrest in Paris, sir, d'Hubert approached me with—a certain proposition.'

'What proposition?' the Comte demanded, looking stern.

'Sir, forgive me, but I swear I am speaking the truth. At first he spoke kindly to me, inquiring if I liked my work and if you paid me well. Then,' Distel paused, glancing across at Suzanne, 'he asked if I had any particular wish or ambition I longed to fulfil. I was surprised by his apparent interest. On previous occasions, he had always ignored me.'

'Continue, Monsieur Distel,' commanded the Comte, his expression increasingly grim.

'I—I suppose I was slightly flattered by his interest.' Distel's young face reddened. 'I told him I wished to be married but could not afford to wed, as the young lady was also impecunious. Then he hinted, most strongly...'

'Well, Monsieur?'

'He suggested that if I were to mention in certain quarters that you, Monsieur le Comte, were involved in a plot to aid the King and Queen out of France, then I should receive handsome remuneration.'

There was a moment of tense silence, then the Comte said heavily: 'Well, Distel, I believe you, for I had suspected as much myself, but it is hard to face the fact that someone whom one has trusted could act so treacherously. But yes, now I must face it.'

'Oh, what dastardly wickedness!' Annabelle burst out. 'But I can believe it too, and I fear his motive was to gain early control of Camoret through marriage to me. Also he spoke most strangely of—revenge.'

The Comte gave her a startled look.

'What mean you? What did he say? His exact words, if you please.'

'Well, *mon oncle*, he said that "to bring me to heel and break my spirit" would make his revenge all the sweeter. I could not understand his meaning at all.'

The Comte looked suddenly haggard and old.

'I believe I do. It has to do with a personal matter. I fear he wishes to be revenged upon me.'

They all gazed at him but he appeared lost in thought. Annabelle said: 'You mean that if you died, or were shut away in prison...?'

'Then his plan would not have miscarried,' broke in the Comte.

'He reckoned without one thing,' the girl said slowly. 'My own feelings had changed. I had outgrown that somewhat foolish infatuation I had for him once. His behaviour towards me when he came here convinced me that he is vain and greedy. Ruthless, too! Uncle, he tried to have you *murdered*!'

'I fear that is not too strong a word. But none of us may return to Camoret at present. Even if it is not confiscated by the State, the unrest in France grows daily, and noble families are in increasing danger.'

'Where is the Marquis now?' Distel asked.

'I—believe he has gone to London,' Annabelle said with some hesitation. 'He swore he would return and force me to marry him. I should prefer to discuss the matter alone with you, uncle.'

Distel stood up.

'Then if Mademoiselle Dupont will come for a stroll in the garden ...?'

Blushing, Suzanne also rose.

'One moment,' Annabelle said. 'Later, we must speak of employment for you here. Nothing can repay you for saving my uncle's life, but there is an unoccupied cottage on the estate which you may care to use.'

'Mademoiselle, my most grateful thanks.'

Suzanne laid a hand shyly on his arm and they went outside together. Standing between the rosebeds, Suzanne withdrew her hand.

'Is it true, Monsieur? Are you in some organisation sworn to rescue *aristos*?'

'Not necessarily aristocrats only, Suzanne. Anyone mistreated by the new régime. That is all I may tell you. We are bound by vows of secrecy.'

'And Captain André is the leader?' Suzanne looked thoughtful.

'He is, and an extremely brave and resourceful

man. He takes the main risks himself on every occasion.' Distel's eyes glowed with hero-worship.

'That day in the woods, it was arranged that he should meet us?'

'He had expressed a particular wish to meet Mademoiselle Annabelle. It was arranged that if any acute emergency arose, and either the Comte or she were in real danger, then I must send a message, and if I could, bring them to *The Swift*. Unfortunately the Comte was taken before I could prevent it.'

Suzanne began walking on slowly, and he went with her.

'Could you not have contrived *some* word to re-assure us?' she asked presently.

'I could not. I had to keep my vow not to appear connected with André. I knew it was my duty to return at once to Paris and begin making plans to rescue the Comte.'

There was a pause.

'Milady Solange thinks you deserted us from cowardice.'

It was Distel's turn to stop. They had entered one of the yew walks and were now hidden from observation from the house. He put a hand beneath her chin and raised her face so that she must look at him. Her lips were trembling.

'Do *you* think that, Suzanne?'

'No, Monsieur,' she whispered. 'That I could never believe.'

'Thank you, *chérie*. Suzanne, ma *petite*, you know I love you. While I was often in danger of capture, even of losing my life, I could not ask you to wed me. That was the main reason; not only our poor circumstances, for I do not think you would mind marrying a man who was not wealthy?'

'No, sir, I would not,' the girl murmured, lashes lying on flushed cheeks.

'Now I am safe, for we are discontinuing our work in France, at least for a time. You heard Miss Annabelle offer me employment here, and a place to live. Little one, will you marry me here in England, and very soon?'

'Oh yes, Gilbert, I will,' she whispered. 'I have been so miserable, but now I know the truth, I am so very proud and happy.'

'May you always remain so,' Distel said, and pulling her hard against him, kissed her quivering mouth.

Left alone with the Comte, Annabelle was trying to decide how best to begin telling him about Lockwood. She was afraid it might enrage him. He had already bestowed Camoret on her, although she intended to assure him that it would remain his property during his life-span. Whoever she married must become Camoret's eventual master, but his ideal dream that that person should be his godson had now been shattered, and she had no wish to add to his anxieties.

On the other hand, he already obviously admired and approved of André. How much should she tell him of her own relationship with the mysterious French captain? There was little as yet that she could tell to *anyone*. When would André return? Would he come to claim her openly as he had promised? Did she actually hope he would, for now, her own mind was clouded by a strange suspicion.

This, more than anything else, dominated her thoughts, and her uncle was in a position to confirm or dispel her fears. She was about to speak when the Comte said harshly: 'So Gaspard spoke to you of "revenge", but you did not understand what he meant?'

'No, uncle. How could I?'

'Perhaps he has some reason to hate me. It is possible he may have come by—certain knowledge that would be bitter as gall to a man of his arrogant pride.'

Annabelle gazed at him in eager inquiry, but he appeared undecided whether to say more. At last she said quietly: 'You have had a wonderful escape, and it would seem that we owe much to this Captain André.'

'Indeed we do.'

'It was dark when I encountered him. How does he look?'

'Tall and well-set-up, though as Distel remarked to me, he has some difficulty in retaining his anonymity.'

Annabelle caught her breath.

'Such unusual eyes,' continued the Comte. 'Striking! Exceptionally beautiful in a man.'

'What colour are they?' Annabelle managed to ask, keeping her voice steady.

Before the Comte could answer, the door opened suddenly. Solange stood on the threshold, Trecarey immediately behind her. At sight of her brother, she uttered a small shriek.

'Henri! You are safe! You are here!'

They embraced, kissing each other on either cheek, French fashion.

'Solange, my dear sister, I have had a miraculous escape.'

Then, of course, Mr Trecarey had to be introduced, and once again the Comte told his story. Annabelle sat trying to steady her shaking nerves. The all-important question still remained unanswered, the fear unassuaged. In the end it was her mother, pink-cheeked with excitement, who exclaimed ecstatically: 'Oh, I am quite overcome by the drama of it all! I am so intrigued to know how we may discover this French captain and offer him our thanks.'

'Distel may know where he can be found,' remarked the Comte. 'If not, providing he is in this country, I cannot think he will be hard to trace. He has one remarkable feature.'

'What is that, *mon frère*?'

'His eyes,' said the Comte de Camoret. 'An amazingly golden hazel colour. Quite unusual and easy to recall. Anyone who has seen them would be likely to remember them.'

CHAPTER
EIGHT

As soon as she could, Annabelle slipped away from the drawing-room and went upstairs to her bedroom. Her mind and feelings were in turmoil. The extraordinary suspicion that had first entered her head on the afternoon following her last encounter with André, when she had again visited the priest, seemed confirmed by what the Comte had told them. He had described André's eyes as 'striking', a 'remarkable golden hazel'. Lockwood's eyes! Surely *two* men could not possess eyes of such unusual shade? Could it really be that Major Lockwood and her beloved captain were one and the same person? If so, then why had André concealed his true identity from her? The answer seemed sickeningly obvious.

Lockwood wanted Sarne. Even more, he desired control of her grandmother's forty thousand pounds. He knew she must loathe and despise the very name of Lockwood so he had cheated, sought to intrigue and charm her into loving him, counting on the strength of her feelings for him to bind her to him even after she finally discovered who he was.

A giant wave of misery and anger engulfed her. If it were true, if Lockwood and André were the same man, then how could she possibly believe he really loved her? The scene on the bridge, his tender, whispered words, the passionate sweetness of his kisses, had all been a sham: nothing but a piece of clever acting on his part, calculated to enslave her senses and make her adore him.

Annabelle sank on to the bed, covering her face with her hands. She felt utterly humiliated, but far worse, beneath the rage and sense of disillusionment a desperate aching sadness swamped her heart. For she *did* love him. Cheat and liar he might be towards her, but was he not also a most courageous, unselfish man, willing to risk his life for others? A man whose undeniable attraction she had felt even when she knew him by the hated name of Lockwood?

Yes, she must admit it to herself; face up to it. Even then she had found him attractive, and when she remembered the feel of his arms about her, the smooth grain of his cheek pressed on hers, his mouth on hers, hot tears trickled between her fingers.

Oh, he had found it very easy to deceive her! She burned afresh at the memory. How amused he must have felt, acting the part of mystery lover, beguiling her into submission. She had whispered: 'I love you,' to a man she thought she had never actually seen. How wild and foolish of her! How very, very stupid to have let him sway her emotions so easily. Now, how utterly wretched she felt.

And yet she owed him the Comte's freedom, almost certainly her uncle's life. For even if a reprieve from execution had been granted eventually, she knew that a man of the Comte de Camoret's pride, yes, and luxurious habits of living, would soon have had his spirit broken by the rigours of perpetual imprisonment. She felt sure he would not have survived for long.

If André were indeed Lockwood, then he was also a brave and resourceful man. With incredible daring, he had entered the lion's den and snatched a victim from its jaws. No wonder Gilbert Distel's eyes glistened with admiration when he spoke of his leader. In her innocence, she thought it strange that one man could be a composite of qualities; heroic, humorous, tender, yet also, apparently, ruthless and calculating.

Suddenly another thought struck her. Lockwood wanted Sarne and her inheritance. He had been forced to take on Sir Julian's debts, but he had been honest enough to see them promptly paid in full. He had sold his home to do so; placed his mother and sisters in an inferior position which must have galled him. Surely a man of such obvious physical magnetism and charm—when he chose to exert it—could have found an easier way, by the means he was now hoping to employ to recoup his losses—marriage with an heiress? The duel might have caused a scandal at the time, but Lockwood came of good family. Annabelle knew quite well, having Solange for a mother, that many a society mother would be willing enough to turn a blind eye to some irregularity of behaviour in order to secure a husband for her daughter.

If he had so wished, Marcus Lockwood should have had no trouble in finding a wealthy wife who could have paid his debts for him.

He had not done so. Instead, he had involved himself in daring and dangerous schemes to rescue foreigners from persecution. Why? For the sheer excitement of it, or for a brave ideal?

Did he, perhaps, want her potential wealth not for his own selfish purposes, but to help finance his 'missions' into France? To aid terrified refugees, fleeing to save their lives? The assignments he undertook must cost a lot. How were they paid for, she wondered.

These new ideas gave her much food for thought and dried her tears. More than ever, she was intrigued by the personality of the French captain, who might very well also be the English major. At whatever cost to herself, she found she wanted to know a great deal more about him.

Then she remembered Gaspard. If Lockwood had been in France during the past two weeks, organising the Comte's rescue, then d'Hubert could not have found and fought with him. What, then, had Gaspard been doing for the last fortnight? Well, at least he had not been back to Sarne to trouble her. She wondered if she might hope he had abandoned all idea of trying to persuade her to become his wife.

Perhaps having had time to reflect, he had now accepted that it was useless to try and press the matter. Annabelle felt tolerably secure. Father Martin would never agree to her being forced into marriage with a man she loathed. Also, Gaspard did not yet know that her uncle was in England, free. But if the Marquis reappeared, she had no doubt that the Comte would show him short shrift. They might not be able to prove Gaspard's treachery, but the Comte would have no further dealings with his godson.

She still felt sick at heart that André might have treated her with perfidy, but until she had final proof, she must hide her feelings from the rest of the household. The ancient and proud blood of Camoret beat in her veins too. She would summon that pride to her aid now, and not let anyone guess her unhappy perplexity.

With this resolve, she got up and went to look in the ewer by the washstand. It still contained a little water from earlier in the day, grown cold. She poured it into the basin and laved her face and hands. Its cool touch bathed away the tear-stains from her cheeks, and she completed the transformation back to normality by a light dusting of powder with a rabbit's foot. Then she took up a comb and rearranged her fair curls.

Looking in the mirror, she had just decided she was satisfied by her appearance when someone tapped on the door. It was Suzanne, and entirely changed from the wan creature who had been haunting the Manor since their return from France. Suzanne's cheeks were rosy with happiness, her brown eyes sparkling with all their old mischief.

'Oh Mees Annabelle,' she said in careful English, 'forgive if I intrude. I am so very 'appy.' And then, lapsing into joyous French, 'Ah, I cannot express myself in a foreign tongue! I wish you to be the first to know my news.'

Annabelle held out both her hands. 'You have come to tell me that you and Monsieur Distel are betrothed?'

'Yes, yes! Is it not heavenly? He has explained everything to me. He begged forgiveness for having caused me sorrow. He—he declared he loves me, and wants us to be married at once.'

'Dearest Suzanne, I am so glad for you.'

'It is your doing, Annabelle. You have made it possible by promising to employ him here, and even giving him a house. There is no *reason*, is there, why we should not be married very soon?' Suzanne asked with a sudden note of anxiety.

'None whatever. The cottage I spoke of is in good repair. All it needs is some furnishings, and those can easily be arranged. Father Martin can perform the nuptial Mass as soon as Distel requests him.'

'Oh ... I can hardly believe it is all true!'

Annabelle smiled, albeit a trifle wanly herself, and Suzanne noticed. She looked closely at her benefactor.

'What is wrong? Is something troubling you?' And then, accusingly: 'Annabelle, you have been crying?'

Annabelle flushed.

'Is it very noticeable? You must not tell anyone you found me like this, especially not Mama. Promise, Suzanne.'

'Of course I shall not. But what is the matter? Can I help? If you wish to confide what is troubling you, you may be certain I shall not repeat it.'

'I—I cannot tell you. I cannot tell *anyone* as yet.'

Suzanne said nothing for a moment, then she came close.

'Is it because he—Captain André—has not come back? Gilbert says he is here in England, but remained in Dover to look after some other *emigrés* who travelled with them on *The Swift*. Your uncle did not know that André was also on board.'

Annabelle looked up quickly.

'But you did not tell Distel about my seeing André near the chapel that night, and—and what passed between us?'

'No, Mademoiselle, certainly I did not. From now on, I shall keep no secrets from Gilbert myself, but I would never break my promise and tell him yours.'

'Oh, Suzanne, I implore you to forgive me,' Annabelle cried. 'I do treat you so unkindly, and I know you are entirely to be trusted. It is just that I am so distraught ...' She broke off, tears trembling near the surface again.

'Would it not ease your mind to tell me?' Suzanne murmured gently.

'I cannot, truly. My—my fears may yet prove unfounded, but I do not think they will.'

Suzanne looked at her with compassion but said

nothing. Annabelle swallowed hard and managed to
steady her voice.

'Once again, I beg you to be patient and forgive me.
Presently, I shall tell you everything, and I may well
need a true friend then.'

'You may always count on me for that,' the French
girl said, then went on with a change of tone: 'It is my
turn to comfort and sustain you. It is almost time
for supper. I have come to help you change your
gown.'

'I am not at all hungry. I could not eat anything.'
Annabelle moved restlessly about the room. 'Please
tell them all I have the headache and have retired
early. Tell Mama I am asleep. Do not let her come to
see me. Tomorrow, I shall feel able to face them
again.'

Suzanne nodded and gave a small puzzled sigh.

'Shall I make you a soothing posset?'

'No, thanks. I think I may go to the chapel for a
while and pray. The evening air might cool my head.'

'Are you feeling ill?'

'No, no, I am perfectly well. Do not fuss, Suzanne.
And then, with contrition: 'Oh, there I go again
snapping at you needlessly, my poor Suzanne! You
had best leave me alone. I am not fit company for
anyone. But I am genuinely happy for you and Mon
sieur Distel. Tomorrow, when I am myself again, we
will start making plans for your wedding.'

After the French girl had gone, still looking dis
turbed, Annabelle went to the window and flung it
open. Cool air gushed across her hot face. It was
nearing dusk, and a slender moon, newly risen, was
casting a sheen on the dewy grass and flowers in the
darkening garden. Oh, how hard it was to be so much
in love and yet unable to trust one's beloved!

'Trust me,' he had said. 'I beseech you to believe in me.'

Annabelle had believed in him completely, but now the serpent of doubt had wormed its way into her mind and filled her with torment. She decided she would go down to the chapel and strive to rediscover peace of mind in that quiet and holy precinct.

'Wait upon events,' Father Martin had counselled her. She had tried to do that, but she had lost her faith.

She took a light grey summer cloak from her closet and slipped it on, drawing the hood up over her blonde hair. She did not want to be observed crossing the garden. Her mother and uncle believed her to be in her room, and if she were discovered out of doors, inevitably there would be curiosity and questions to parry. She opened her door and stood listening. Down in the well of the house she could hear sounds of movement, the clink of dishes. The servants would be occupied now in kitchen and dining-room, preparing and serving the meal. She could slip out by using the servants' staircase at the back.

A few minutes later, she was outside. She rounded the side of the house and moved quietly along the edge of the lawn towards the woodland path that led to the bridge, the priest's house and the chapel. Before stepping in among the trees, she paused and looked back. The dining-room curtains were not drawn and she could see inside the room. She could see her mother, the Comte and Mr Trecarey seated at the long oaken table; candlelight sparkling on glass and silver. So Mr Trecarey had been invited to remain for dinner! The Comte must approve of him.

She had never really given it much thought, but Carne owned considerable wealth in its own right. Her paternal grandfather had been something of a collector. The house contained many pieces of expensive furniture, and collectors' items; Chinese vases, exquisitely hand-painted, jade and gold, and elegant wood and ivory carvings. Even without her grandmother's money, she could claim to be a rich young woman, she thought wryly. No wonder Lockwood was anxious to seek ownership of the manor.

With a sigh, she turned to hurry along the path. It was a quiet evening. Even the small river seemed to be flowing more softly than usual, and tonight no frogs set up a lively croaking among the reeds to greet her. She paused on the bridge and peered into the shadows. If only André would speak her name as before, come to her and drive out all her fears.

She must not think like that! She must no longer allow herself to believe in his vows of love, even though her whole being cried out that she wanted to be his wife, whatever the circumstances. She could be, if she chose, but at what expense to herself? The expense of her own self-respect!

Ahead, she could see a faint flickering glow inside the chapel. Father Martin never let the candles die. Nearer at hand, she observed another light in the priest's cottage. He would be eating his supper now, probably one of his herbal stews, and bread of his own baking. She could picture him, a book propped on the table before him to study while he ate, peering at it with his rheumy old eyes in the dim light!

A sudden rustle came in the bushes beyond the stream, and her heart leapt. André ...?

Then fright jolted through her. A figure lunged out of the darkness; heavy boots thumped on the bridge. Annabelle turned to run, opening her mouth to scream. Something thick and stifling came down over her head, blotting out the moonshine. Rough hands seized her, lifted ... She was flung over a powerful shoulder, hanging head down, choking, throttling in the folds of woollen cloth stinking of horse sweat.

If Annabelle had been the swooning kind, she would have fainted then from sheer terror, but she remained conscious. She was being carried, bumped and jostled as her captor ran with her. Mingled with the frantic thudding of her own blood in her ears, she could hear his harsh breaths.

She tried to scream, but the thick material, entangled with the hood of her cloak, was nearly choking her, pressed into her face. She could feel the man's arm, an iron band about her thighs. Jerked and shaken like that, she could not think, only feel. She was semi-paralysed by shock and fright. What was going to happen to her? Was she to be ravished, *murdered*, her tortured body tossed into some ditch?

Again she tried to shriek, but the blanket smothered the sound. She could hardly breathe. Hot and giddy, she struggled feebly, but his arm only tightened round her legs and he muttered: 'Quiet, lady, and you'll not get 'urt.'

She concentrated then on trying to get her breath, keep her head and not vomit. Suddenly, they stopped. She was lowered, none too gently, into an upright position, the cloth still over her. She would have fallen, but hands held her, and through the muffling blanket she heard new sounds; the clink of harness and the stamping of a restless horse. Next moment, she was lifted again and propelled forward, then half-thrown down on to a seat. A carriage! It must be a carriage! A second later, it jerked into movement.

Annabelle struggled up and fought her way out of the enveloping blanket. She was gasping for breath, it was totally dark; the carriage blinds must be down.

Bounced and thrown about, she almost fell on the floor, but managed to grip the edge of the seat. Next moment, her heart nearly stopped. In the blackness a hand grasped her arm.

'Who—who is it?' she whispered, hardly able to speak from fear. Even as she spoke, she knew. A familiar odour assailed her nostrils; the smell of stale perfume.

'Well, my Lady Arrogance,' a voice said softly and mockingly, close to her ear, 'who should it be but your future husband, come to claim his rights?'

CHAPTER
NINE

'GASPARD!'

The girl shrank away, leaning back into the corner as far from him as she could. Now she could dimly discern his figure in the darkness.

'Yes, *ma chère* Annabelle, it is Gaspard.' He sounded considerably amused. 'I must ask your pardon for having had you used so roughly. On this occasion it could not be avoided.'

'You ... you ...' She was struggling to find words, her fear overwhelmed by an uprush of sheer blazing fury. 'How *dare* you? Just what do you think you are playing at? What do you hope to gain by this—this ...'

'Playing?' he interrupted her in smooth tones. 'Now why should you imagine I am in playful mood?' His voice hardened, lost its note of mockery. 'This is no play-acting, I assure you. It is in deadly earnest. I mean to make you my wife, by fair means or foul. The choice can be yours.'

'You are abducting me?' she gasped, hardly able to credit it.

'Unfortunately such a drastic step would seem to be necessary, as I am persuaded now that you would never consent to wed me of your own free will.'

'Most certainly I would not,' she cried furiously. 'And make no mistake, sir, this course of action will do you no good either. Have I not told you already? Nothing in heaven or earth will ever force me into marriage with you. I have found out what you are.'

'I am sure that such haughty defiance must become
your looks,' he said, sounding coldly amused again,
'but I should not be quite so sure of your ground, if I
were in your position.'

'What do you mean?'

'It is I who have the whip-hand, is it not? Who will
aid you? Your foolish mother? Dear Aunt Solange is
scarcely likely to do more than have a notable fit of the
vapours once your disappearance is discovered.
Pretty little Dupont? Oh, I am aware of her devotion
to you, but how do you imagine she can help you
now?'

Annabelle was opening her mouth to tell him
fiercely that her uncle the Comte and Monsieur Distel
would not let any stone be left unturned to find her,
when she remembered that he did not know that they
were safe and in England. She shut it again firmly, and
hoped he might sense scorn in her silence.

'What a pity your uncle the Comte de Camoret is
not here to command any search party,' the Marquis
continued mockingly, almost as if he had sensed her
thoughts. 'He is safely locked away in France, if he has
not already lost his head. I have seen to that. His dog
of a servant is also still in France. No, my dear
Annabelle, the choice, as I said, is yours. If you refuse
to accept me as your husband willingly, then there are
other means by which you may be brought to heel.'

The harshness of his tone shot a chill through her.
For the first time since realising whose coach she
shared, she felt a doubt as to whether she could handle
the situation. But she was determined to hide her
anxiety.

'You had better make your meaning clear,' she said
haughtily. 'You threaten me, but with what validity?'

'I think you understand me very well. You would

scarcely wish to return to Sarne unwed after a night or two spent in my company.'

She gave a small gasp. 'You call yourself a gentleman and yet suggest *that*!'

'If you refuse my overtures, there is always Grimshaw,' he responded imperturbably.

'Grimshaw?'

'My new servant. A somewhat uncouth fellow, I fear, but useful.' He leaned forward suddenly and tapped with his cane upon the roof of the carriage. 'Slow down a trifle, Grimshaw, my good man. We are not being pursued. There is no need to shake the lady quite so much.'

He leaned back once more. 'With all this rattling about it must be difficult for you to think or make decisions, Annabelle. Yes,' he went on, reverting to his normal bored tones, 'Grimshaw is certainly useful. A touch crude in his manners, as I believe you have already discovered. I fear he may have dealt with you more roughly than I intended, but then he is not accustomed to handling young *ladies*.'

He paused, but Annabelle, beginning to appreciate his full meaning, was speechless with horror and disgust.

'Grimshaw has one very useful attribute,' continued d'Hubert in quite a pleasantly conversational tone. 'He will do absolutely anything for money. He has known true poverty, you see; he was bred in the London gutters. He dislikes hunger and cold as much as anyone, and means to ensure that he does not suffer them again. I have assured him that he will not, if he serves me with absolute obedience. As I was remarking, should you prefer his attentions to mine ...?'

'You are utterly contemptible,' Annabelle interrupted in a quiet voice.

'I imagined you might think so, but it is of no consequence. A woman's thoughts are of no importance to me. Women have but one function—to obey their husbands and provide heirs. If you do *your* duty properly, my dear, we shall have no quarrel.'

Annabelle could not reply. Emotions whirled inside her, but instinctively she knew it would be useless to rail at him. He was ruthless, merciless, entirely insulated by his cloak of vanity to either scorn or pleading. Not that she would ever plead with him. She would die first rather than give him such satisfaction. Striving to keep her voice from shaking, she managed presently to ask, 'Where are you taking me?'

'I suppose there is no reason why I should not tell you. Have you been curious as to what I have been doing since our last meeting?'

'I have given it scarcely a single thought.'

'A pity, for my actions closely concerned yourself.'

'Indeed?' she queried coldly.

'Yes indeed, my dear girl. Well, I shall tell you even though you pretend disinterest. I have obtained the hire of a house. An old place—it has not been occupied for years. Also, I understand, it is eschewed by the local people. Superstition is rife among the lower classes, as I am sure you know.'

'And why should people fear this place you have found, wherever it may be?'

'Ah, so I have managed to prick your interest after all. Apparently, a particularly gruesome murder took place there some years ago. Local rumour has it that the place is haunted by the unquiet spirit of the murdered girl. It is, however, excellent for my purpose, for it stands alone some two miles out along the coast from Dover.'

Dover! Annabelle's confused and frightened mind

reacted with a glimmer of hope. Suzanne had said that *The Swift* was still at Dover and that André was aboard. André? Lockwood? Could she expect his help? But hope died as swiftly as it had risen. How could she hope to get free and find him?

She gripped her hands together in her lap and tried to think. She had some slight advantage in that Gaspard believed that the Comte and Distel were still in France. He thought there was no one who could possibly seek for her. But they would not be likely to discover her loss for hours, perhaps not until tomorrow. She was supposed to be in her room, sleeping off a sick headache. She had given orders not to be disturbed. By tomorrow, heaven alone knew what fate might have overtaken her.

With a tremendous effort, she forced herself to speak calmly.

'How can it benefit you to make me marry you now? We cannot return to France, either of us. By the time we may, the Château de Camoret might well be lost for good. Years may pass before we can go back. Everything has altered.'

'For the moment, yes, but I cannot believe that it will last. Shall France be ruled by a pack of starving dogs? No, before long this anarchy will be controlled, the rebels punished and the power of the nobles restored. I am convinced of that. It has been the rule in France for centuries, and a few madmen are not going to change the whole of France's heritage by chopping off some heads. 'Tis merely a matter of patience for a few more months. Meanwhile, do you think I shall allow some crude Englishman to steal that which by rights is mine? Camoret should be mine. No, Annabelle, you are the right wife for me. Your lineage matches mine, better than you know. You are a fit mother for my heirs, and as I told you at our last meeting, you will make a perfect ornament for my house.'

The condescension in his tone maddened her. She sat biting her lips against the flow of angry words that would only serve to make him mock her more. If she were to have any chance at all of escaping from this desperate situation, it was essential for her to keep a cool head and her courage.

Even as she thought this, he leaned towards her, feeling for her hand, and murmured: 'Come, my foolish one, why continue to defy me? You are trapped. Give in with a good grace. Once we are married we can make a fine life here in England for the present. Your manor needs a master, and you a husband. As that man, I shall be welcomed into English society. Why struggle against the decree of Fate?'

She snatched her hand away, pushing at him wildly.

'Fate? It is not Fate, but your greedy will. Do not touch me! I—I loathe and despise you. I shall *not* be your wife.'

She heard the angry hiss of his breath and waited, poised, tense with determination to try and fight him with all her strength if he tried to take hold of her again. Then he said icily, 'Pardon, Milady Virtue. I perceive that I try to go too fast. You may have a few hours to reflect upon your position. If by tomorrow you are not compliant to my wish, you know the alternative. 'Twould be a pity to let an uncouth creature such as Grimshaw take first bite of the apple, but if it must take that to bring you into line ...'

He left the sentence unfinished.

Shivering, Annabelle sat huddled in her corner of the coach. She was pathetically determined not to let him know how frightened she felt. When she was able to control her voice, she said coldly, 'Your threats leave me unmoved, sir. If you consider yourself a fine example of French nobility, then I can feel nothing but pity and contempt for you. Perhaps you will answer me one question? You spoke of the Comte, my uncle; you declared that you had "seen to it" that he was "safely locked away". Will you explain your meaning?'

She reckoned that his overweening vanity and love of power over anyone weaker than himself would induce him to tell her. There would be no witnesses to his confession, but she wanted to hear him admit the extent of his treachery; treachery to one who had always treated him with generosity and affection. She was not disappointed.

'Yes, now I shall tell you. Do you know what it means to hate, Annabelle? Do you understand what it could mean to a boy who adored his mother and believed in the pride of his family name, to discover that he had, in fact, no blood right to that name? That his mother was not chaste as he had thought, but—a whore, who had cuckolded the man he believed was his father?'

Annabelle gave a small gasp. In the darkness she heard the angry rasp of his breathing. He went on:

'As a child, I quickly realised that the Duc disliked me. Why, I could not understand. Constantly he belittled me, humiliated me. He took every chance to shame and humiliate my mother too, and I hated him for it. And then, when I was fifteen years old, I learned the truth. One day, in a fit of rage, he accused her of having been unfaithful, declared he had always suspected I was not his true son.'

Understanding was beginning to dawn in Annabelle's mind.

'And you think ... my uncle ...?'

'I taxed my mother to tell me the truth. She admitted it, but would not tell me the name of the man who had been her lover—who was, in fact, my father. From that day on, I could scarcely bear to look at her. My one wish was to discover the man's identity, but it was not until last year, when she lay dying, that she finally told me. Yes, Annabelle, it was Camoret.'

He almost choked over the name. 'So you see, my dear, that I have a special right to own the château. For a year I have planned revenge upon the Comte—planned to see him humiliated as I have been. If I could ruin him and take control of his estates through marriage to you, so much the better. Poor fool, he played right into my hands by actually suggesting our union.'

He laughed harshly.

'It was easy enough to arrange for his arrest. A few greedy palms crossed with silver, and half-a-dozen witnesses were ready to speak against him and swear him guilty of aiding Louis's escape.'

Annabelle was too appalled by the blatancy of his perfidy to answer. Her uncle had been right when he said that certain knowledge would prove bitter as gall to someone of Gaspard's pride. As if reading her thoughts, he continued:

'It will be an added pleasure to humiliate *you*, my dear; the one person for whom I think my godfather really cares.'

Annabelle ignored him. She sat in silence, but her mind was fully active again, considering and discarding possibilities.

Back at Sarne, Solange and the gentlemen completed their meal and Solange rose to leave them to their port and smoking. Throughout, there had been a most amicable atmosphere, and she had been much gratified to observe how well Henri took to her new neighbour. She knew that her brother could be a little over-conscious of his high Camoret lineage at times. A simple Cornish squire was not entirely in his class, but perhaps his recent distressing experiences had given Henri greater tolerance. At first there had been some air of reserve on her brother's part, but Mr Trecarey had shown such excellent tact in his handling of the situation. She had felt quite overcome by admiration for the manner he had shown towards the noble Comte de Camoret; exactly the correct amount of deference but without any trace of sycophancy.

They had discovered a mutual interest in the collection of unusual snuff-boxes. Mr Trecarey evidently owned several of early design and he invited the Comte to go over to Winkworth Grange to view them at a suitable time. The Comte had graciously accepted. They had discussed the subject at some length, and Solange might have felt a little neglected without Annabelle to talk to, if she had not been so pleased to see them getting along well together.

In the drawing-room, she rang for Suzanne. Henri had informed her of Annabelle's wish that Suzanne should no longer be treated as a servant.

Solange was not quite sure whether she approved. Suzanne was generally a docile little thing, and it was not her fault that fate had left her unprovided for, but she could show signs of impertinence now and then. It was particularly noticeable when Solange felt obliged to criticise Annabelle. Suzanne was almost absurdly loyal to her friend and benefactor. Still, they were of an age, and young girls were rather prone to band together against parental authority. It was a known fact. In the old days, she had often heard friends complain of the wilfulness of their daughters.

Solange had not felt obliged to suggest that Suzanne and Distel should join them for dining. After all, they could not be called *entirely* equal to the Comte de Camoret and his family. So they had dined in another room with the Proudfoots. Suzanne and Distel were to be married, she recalled. Henri had already approved the match and Solange agreed that it was a sound idea. Really, it was quite amazing to reflect that that quiet, unassuming, *dull* young man, her brother's secretary, should actually have been leading a dramatic double life ever since they had known him. Undoubtedly, he had played a large part in the rescue of dear Henri, so if he wished to marry the little Dupont girl, then that would provide an excellent solution to Suzanne's future and stabilise her place in the household.

When Suzanne came in and curtsied, Solange nodded approvingly. Good! The chit was not giving herself airs because of her promotion in status.

'Suzanne, it is a pity that my daughter is feeling unwell. Do you think I should go up and see her?'

'Mees Annabelle said she wished to sleep, milady. She asked not to be disturbed.'

'So we had better abide by her wish.' Solange felt relieved. She detested a sickroom atmosphere unless it were her own. 'You are satisfied it is nothing serious? Merely a headache?'

'I think so, but I will look in on her when I go to my room,' Suzanne said.

'Yes, do that, if you please. Or you might go up now, to make entirely certain she does not require anything.'

'I will do zat, milady.'

'I am pleased to see you practising your English,'

Solange said graciously. 'It is not too difficult a language to learn, really. My poor husband taught me how to speak it when I was little older than you are now. I believe you are soon to wed my brother's secretary?'

'Yes, milady.' Suzanne blushed.

'Then I wish you both all happiness. Now, please go to visit my daughter and make certain she is resting.'

Suzanne curtsied again and left the room. Solange patted her dove-grey curls and spread the skirts of her wine-coloured evening gown, making sure that she would present a charmingly domesticated picture when Mr Trecarey came in with Henri, but a few moments later Suzanne reappeared, looking much troubled.

'Pardon, milady, but I think I had better tell you—Mademoiselle Annabelle is not in her room.'

'Not in her room?' Solange repeated.

'She has not been in bed at all.' Suzanne hesitated. 'She did say she might visit the chapel for a time.'

'Well, that is where she has gone, no doubt.'

'But, milady, that was more than three hours ago.' Solange wrinkled her brow.

'Three hours? That does seem a little strange. Perhaps she is with Father Martin?'

'As late as this? It is nearly eleven. The priest retires early, as a rule,' Suzanne pointed out.

Solange began feeling mildly anxious and consequently annoyed. What in the world could Annabelle be doing so inconveniently at this time of night?

'What are you suggesting, Suzanne? Surely ...'

'Shall I ask Monsieur Distel to go to the priest's house and see if she is there?'

'Yes, please do that immediately.'

Fifteen minutes later, the whole household was set

by the ears. Annabelle could not be found. Father
Martin had answered Distel's knock in his nightrobe.
No, he had seen no sign of Miss Annabelle since
yesterday. She was not in the chapel. The manor
house was searched from top to bottom, and Suzanne
noticed that Annabelle's favourite summer cloak was
not on its customary hook. So the grounds were
searched too, by torchlight, and near the boundary
wall behind the chapel a servant found a lace handkerchief. Beyond the wall, in the soft earth, were
definite hoof-prints and signs that a carriage had
rested there recently.

Consternation reigned at Sarne. Solange did as the
Marquis had predicted and threw a violent fit of hysterics.

Behind the drawn blinds of the Marquis d'Hubert's
coach, Annabelle had no means of knowing when
they passed through Dover, but when they came along
the coast road she heard the sea washing waves on to
the shore, and guessed that they must be nearly at
Gaspard's secret retreat. Soon the horses' hooves
made a different sound, crunching on gravel, and
d'Hubert roused himself.

'Do not attempt anything foolish when you alight.
Grimshaw is fast on his feet and would soon capture
you again. And there is no one to hear you scream.'

Annabelle had no wish for a repeat performance of
the servant's rough handling. She got out of the carriage with as much haughty dignity as she could muster, and stood breathing in the fresh, cool air. It was a
relief from the Marquis's perfumes. In the faint moonlight, she could just make out the edge of an unkempt
lawn backed by trees etched against a starry sky, and
the solid block of the house. At first she thought no

one was within, for the windows were all shuttered and dark, then a door opened at the top of some wide steps and a woman holding a taper peered out.

'Allow me to assist you up the steps, *ma chère*,' murmured the Marquis with mocking courtesy. Annabelle drew her skirts aside ostentatiously and preceded him.

She entered a large bare hall. The woman, a slatternly creature, stood back staring at her with avid interest. She was middle-aged, clad in a dark dress, her hair stuffed untidily in a cap with wisps protruding. D'Hubert said curtly: 'This is Grimshaw's mother, my housekeeper here. She will also act as your servant until after we are married.'

'Or as my gaoler,' Annabelle muttered, returning the woman's hard stare.

The man Grimshaw had followed them up the steps, and by the light from the taper Annabelle saw him for the first time. An uncouth creature indeed, with the kind of low forehead that often denotes a mean intelligence; a thick-lipped mouth and insolently assessing eyes. She wondered if he knew of d'Hubert's threat to permit him to 'bring her to heel', and could hardly control her shudder of revulsion.

She looked away round the empty, carpetless hall, her gaze following the stairs that vanished upward into dense shadow. She began to tremble. She was exhausted by the uncomfortable journey and the hours of strain, and felt her determination to be brave and defiant starting to waver into a desperate fear that she might burst out sobbing, pleading for mercy.

'Is the room prepared for Miss Sarne as I instructed?' the Marquis asked of the housekeeper.

'Yes, sir. I done all you said. Bed's made up, and just one candle on the cupboard top. There's a bit o' fire in the living-room, and a cold collation ready, like you ordered.'

'Give her your cloak,' Gaspard told the girl, swinging his own from his shoulders and handing it to Grimshaw. Annabelle hugged hers around her.

'I prefer to keep mine on. I am chilled from travelling.'

She was not, but instinctively she wanted to hold on to all she possessed, in case it might prove useful later.

The Marquis shrugged, indicating a door on the left, and she went before him into the room. It revealed some signs of comfort. The floor was carpeted; an easy chair was placed near the hearth, and a table was set for two persons beside it. He bowed Annabelle mockingly to a chair.

'Are you hungry, my dear? I confess I am quite famished. I have been too fully occupied today to give much thought to food.'

He poured wine from a carafe on the table and passed her a glass. Momentarily she felt tempted to hurl it back in his face, but such behaviour could only enrage him and perhaps lessen any chance she might gain later of saving herself. She sipped the wine, and its vital warmth helped to still her inner shaking. She had to acknowledge to herself that she too was ravenous. She had not eaten since midday and now it was past midnight. Tired though she was, her healthy young body craved nourishment.

She had decided, however, on a course of action; appearing disdainfully to ignore her kidnapper. When he tried to draw her into conversation, she merely looked through him. At first he seemed amused, but when he continued to behave as though he did not exist, she saw sullen annoyance enter his eyes.

They ate cold roast ham and salad in studied

silence. The girl feared what might happen to her after the meal and was steeling herself to cope with it. But perhaps the Marquis was tired too, for when he had finished eating he sat back, patting his lips in one of his small simulated yawns.

'You are not good company, *ma chère*, but perhaps it is understandable. Doubtless you are somewhat weary after so long a journey?'

'Yes, sir, I am,' Annabelle said, speaking for the first time in half an hour.

'Well, for what remains of the night you may rest. Tomorrow ... shall I tell you, briefly, my plans for the morrow?'

The girl inclined her head.

'Tomorrow we shall receive a visitor. A gentleman of the cloth.'

He paused and she saw that he was watching her with that look of calculating interest she had observed before. He was assessing her reactions. Deliberately she gave none, merely sitting with folded hands, returning his look steadily.

'An *emigré* priest,' he said, 'one who has found life hard since coming to this country. For a consideration, he has agreed to marry us. I shall make certain, before his arrival, that you—will not make difficulties. You understand me?'

She did not reply, merely looked at him, a look of utter scorn and loathing. He got up swiftly and came round the table to stand behind her. She half-rose, defensively, but he took her by the shoulders, forcing her down again, then caught her head between his hands.

With his fingers digging into her skull he said softly, menacingly: 'Be warned, my lady Arrogance. I mean every word I have said. Tomorrow, you will be my wife. It will give me joy to make you grovel, to plead that *I* shall be the one to take you rather than that stable lout who at this moment is guzzling his supper in the kitchen as a pig guzzles in its trough. Let me remind you once more, the choice is yours.'

As Mrs Grimshaw came in, he released her abruptly.

'Take Miss Sarne to her room. Lock her in and bring the key to me here.'

Annabelle got shakily to her feet and went after the woman. As they approached the stairs, the light from the candle Mrs Grimshaw carried flung grotesque shadows on walls and ceiling. Annabelle glanced round wildly. This might be her only chance ... But she saw the heavy bolts drawn across the front door, too heavy to be moved fast. Before she could open them, the woman's shouts would bring Gaspard from the parlour, perhaps that other man from the kitchen quarters.

Then she saw him leaning against the wall beyond the foot of the staircase, watching her ...

She abandoned hope then, and scrambled after Mrs Grimshaw, keeping close to her as they ascended. To her intense relief Grimshaw did not follow them up, but stayed where he was, only pursuing her with that insolent, lascivious look.

Mrs Grimshaw led her along a narrow passage and opened a door at the end, standing aside to let her pass. The room was huge and bare except for a big four-poster bed, one hard-backed chair, and a small bedside cupboard where the single candle offered a little light. Annabelle suddenly remembered the young woman reputed to have been cruelly murdered in this house, and she shivered. Impulsively, she swung to face the housekeeper.

'Mrs Grimshaw,' she whispered frantically, 'do not leave me alone, I—I beg you. I am afraid of what may happen to me later. I have been brought here against my will ...'

' 'Ush, Miss. If they 'ear you ...' Momentarily, the woman's drawn face softened.

'Help me,' Annabelle implored. 'Come back later, when they are asleep ...'

Footsteps crossed the hall below. Mrs Grimshaw's eyes hardened, her mouth snapped shut.

'Sh! I dassn't. 'E's paid me well, and I've the lad to keep. 'Taint easy, gettin' work. Git inside. I can't do nothing.'

She gave Annabelle a sudden push, slammed the door shut, and the key turned in the lock.

CHAPTER
TEN

IN the quiet that followed the grating sound of that
key turning, despair almost overwhelmed Annabelle.
She stood in the centre of the room, hands clenched at
her sides, fighting down surges of panic as she faced
the appalling truth. She was a prisoner. No one had
the slightest inkling where she was. Her uncle, Distel,
André, none could aid her now. She was in the hands
of an utterly ruthless man, a man quite capable of
cold-blooded murder or of raping a defenceless
woman. Gaspard's consuming greed for power might
have received a setback in that circumstances had
forced him to leave France for a time, but he meant to
gain security in England through her, and later
renewed wealth in France, once they could go back.
Any chance of escape from here must depend entirely
on her own ingenuity, and she had but a single night in
which to achieve it.

Many young women might well have been crushed
by such a hopeless prospect, but the acceptance of her
seemingly impossible position had the reverse effect
on Annabelle. It steadied her nerve.

She went to the bed and laid her cloak on it, then
took up the candle to inspect the room. First she went
to listen at the door, but this was an old house, the
walls and doors thick and solid. She could hear
nothing, and had no means of knowing whether Grimshaw had been set to stand guard outside in the passage. Cautiously she tried the door-handle, a strong

knob made of carved brass; uselessly, of course. The door was firmly locked.

The window, then, represented her only chance. Quickly she drew the curtain aside. The window was a hinged casement, lattice-paned. She put out a hand to try the catch, then remembered that if anyone watched below, they would see her outlined against the candlelight. She went back inside the room, replaced the candle by the bed, then slipped behind the thick curtain again. Carefully, she pressed the window latch.

To her great relief, the window opened easily without a creak.

Summer nights are seldom pitch dark, but the radiance cast by the sliver of moon was so slight that she could see very little in the darkness below. She could not gauge the distance to the ground or have any idea of the sort of earth on which she might land were she to attempt the drop. Softly closing the window again, she returned to sit on the edge of the bed and think.

She wished she could estimate better how high this room was from the ground outside. If only she had thought to count the stairs as she came up. Fifteen? Twenty, perhaps. Better to over-estimate. The staircase had been steep and the ceiling of the room below quite high. She decided that the drop must be anything from twenty to twenty-five feet. Much too high to risk jumping, especially as she could not tell how soft the earth might be. Flower-bed soil? Or hard gravel? A broken leg would scarcely benefit her situation.

She thought, with a touch of wry humour for her predicament, how in fairy tales the captured princess usually let down her golden locks for the hero to climb to her rescue. Her own fair curls were barely shoulder-length and, she remembered bitterly, her hero might well prove false. She shut out that thought; it was too depressing. The only practical solution was the obvious one of knotted bed-sheets.

Annabelle jumped up at once to examine them. They were coarse, unbleached linen, suitable only for servant use, and a servant's cotton nightgown was folded beneath the pillow. Gaspard seemed determined to insult her even in minor ways, but she smiled. This time perhaps he had overreached himself. These sheets must prove stronger for holding her weight than the fine lawn to which she was accustomed would have done.

She was about to strip them from the bed and start tying them together when a thought struck her. Suppose Gaspard sent Mrs Grimshaw back to see if she required anything? Or even came himself? Perhaps she might be wiser to get into bed and be ready to feign sleep; she would wait for at least an hour until the household had had time to settle.

It took self-control, for she was desperate to try and get away at once, but she forced herself to get undressed and don the ugly nightgown. Then she sat in the big bed, tense with anxiety. Barely ten minutes later, she was thankful for her caution. She heard the key scrape in the door lock.

In a flash she had blown out the candle and slithered down beneath the coverlet, closing her eyes, but she was rigid with fear. Could it be Mrs Grimshaw? Or Gaspard? Worst of all, could it possibly be the brutish servant, creeping in after his master had retired for the night?

The thought brought her out in a cold perspiration. She lay with every muscle tensed, ready to spring up shrieking for help if hands tried to remove the bedcovers. After an interminable moment, she was conscious of faint light on her eyelids. Whoever it was was standing by the bed, looking down at her.

She strove to keep her breathing regular and calm. Then, just when she felt she could not endure the tension for another instant, the light vanished, and she heard the soft creak of a board nearby.

Tentatively, Annabelle raised her lashes a fraction and caught the retreating outline of a figure nearing the door. Smooth-coated shoulders, wigged head! Gaspard! Thank heaven, he had not given the key to Grimshaw and ordered the man to guard her. A moment later, the door closed almost silently and she heard the key turn again.

Annabelle let out a shuddering sigh. She sat up slowly. The blackness of the room was unnerving, but she allowed a long time to pass before feeling for the brimstone matches and relighting her candle. It was exquisite relief to stare about into the shadowy room and reassure herself that she was indeed the only occupant.

It was torture to her nerves to have to go on waiting, but she made herself do so. The candle was well burnt down before she slipped out of bed and began dressing hurriedly. All her tiredness had vanished now that she was keyed up for action. She stripped off the bed-sheets, but it was not easy for her small slender fingers, unused to rough work of any sort, to knot the harsh linen. She broke a nail in the process, but was finally satisfied that they would hold firm, and tied one end to a bed-post.

It was then that she realised how foolishly optimistic she had been. The bed was some twelve feet from the window, and the sheet rope dangled for perhaps barely five below the window-ledge.

Hands shaking now, Annabelle hauled it in again and fetched the candle, searching in the vicinity of the open window for some place strong enough where she might fasten her makeshift lifeline. There was nothing other than the curtain-rod which she could not hope to reach even by standing on the single chair. In any case, she was not certain that it would have borne even her slight weight. So she must somehow lengthen her rope, but with what? The bed coverlet was made of stiff woven material, much too thick to knot to the sheets. Her petticoats? Thank goodness, skirts were no longer worn hooped or paniered, but her frilled petticoats were flimsy, far too thin to hold her without tearing. There remained only her cloak which might add a few feet. It was far from adequate, but she attached it to the sheet end. Now to pull the bed nearer to the casement without too much noise!

But when she seized hold of one of the posts, she could not make it budge a single inch; it seemed riveted to the floor. She gazed round in despair. The candle was beginning to flicker and waver. Soon it would snuff out altogether, leaving her in complete darkness. Oh, what could she use? The chair was not weighty enough to counterbalance the drag of her body. The bedside cupboard was solid wood; it had no legs to which she could tie the sheet-end.

Then all at once she thought of something. The doorknob! She flew to examine it.

It was made of solid brass and fastened to the door by a number of strong-looking nails. There seemed just sufficient space to try and fasten her rope to the narrower part of the handle. The door stood adjacent to the window, at right angles. Dare she risk it? Sup-

osing Grimshaw *had* been posted outside in the
assage and saw the handle move?

Even in her state of nervous apprehension,
Annabelle thought that this did not seem too prob-
ble. The Marquis thought her safely locked in and
sleep. She felt sure that he would never imagine that
he, a young lady of apparently delicate physique,
would ever have the nerve to attempt what she was
bout to do. He just would not think her capable of
uch foolhardy action.

She hurried back and began trying to undo the sheet
rom the bed-post but she had tugged it so tight that
he experienced real difficulty in loosening it again,
nd broke another nail. Frantically, she struggled with
t. The candle dimmed, wavering; in a few moments,
ll light would be gone. The sheet came loose at last.
Half sobbing with the tension of frustration, she crept
ack to the door. The candle flared slightly and went
ut. At once, the room seemed intensely black.

She had to achieve her object by touch now. She
managed, awkwardly, to double-tie the knot round
he handle, and pulled and tugged with all her strength
o tighten it. Then she felt her way to the window and
pened it again. Cool air flowed in sweetly over her
eated face. It was quite dark outside now. Even the
light moon had gone. Surely it must soon be nearing
dawn, and she still had to find her way to Dover town
nd beseech help from someone.

She could not see the ground at all. She had no
otion of how far she might have to drop when she
eached the end of her sheet rope. Suppose she dam-
ged herself severely? Suddenly she was very much
fraid—pure physical fear. She pushed the window as
vide open as it would go and leaned out, listening
ntently.

There was absolute silence, not a breath of wind in the trees. She could not even hear the far-off hushing of the sea. The night was perfectly calm and still.

Annabelle drew a deep breath and prepared to climb on to the sill. The space was narrow and her skirts bulky, and impatiently she pulled off all her petticoats save one. That helped a little, but even so her dress caught on the window-catch and she heard it rip when she tried to tug it free too carelessly.

Somehow she managed to turn round, facing into the room, and lowered herself gingerly into a kneeling position and then on to her stomach, clinging desperately to the window-frame as she did so. It took real courage to let go and grasp the sheet rope with both hands. Clinging on fiercely, she began awkwardly to slither down.

When her feet came to the end of the material, she still had no idea of how far she had to fall. She hung on wildly, trying to gather enough nerve to make the final drop. Then, without warning, the sheet rope slackened. She fell, landing on soft soil and the sheets flounced down on top of her, half smothering her. Lying entangled, gasping from shock, she knew what must have happened. The knot had slipped off the door-handle!

Well, at least she wasn't hurt. Gingerly she moved, testing her limbs, but no harm had been done at all. Thank the Blessed Virgin for that, she thought, and she crossed herself, whispering one quick 'Ave', then got up cautiously and stared about her.

Now every nerve tensed to hasten her escape, but she had to try and get her bearings. She began bundling the sheets up in her arms. There was no time to try and rescue her cloak; she must hope to conceal the lot under some bush. She could see very little, but the darkness was thinning slightly. Dawn was coming soon, and she must get away quickly. All at once, not far from where she crouched, someone coughed.

Annabelle froze. She could see nothing other than the denser darkness of trees beyond the lawn. Somehow she must reach their shelter, hide. Hardly breathing, heart thudding, she stood clutching her bunch of sheets, and stared round wildly. To her left, at the corner of the house, she discerned a dim, rounded shape. A water butt! Cautiously, she crept towards it. It had no lid. An open butt, and only half full of water! There had been little rain recently. In a second she had deposited her bundle inside, and turned. The cough was repeated, nearer this time.

At that moment, perhaps fifty yards away, she caught sight of a pinpoint of orange light. Just a gleam and it was gone, but she knew what it tokened. Someone standing there, facing in her direction, had drawn on a cheroot!

Annabelle stayed still, clutching at the edge of the water butt. Again came that bright gleam. Obviously the man had not yet seen her, but every second the sky seemed to be growing paler. Very soon objects would become discernible. Panic-stricken, she gazed about. Was she at the front of the house or the back? She must think...! Last night she had noted that they approached the house from the right, so the entrance gate must be somewhere over in that direction.

She tried to visualise the layout of the rooms she had seen, the position of the staircase, and decided that her bedroom had faced towards the back. So this must be the back garden! She must get round to the front and find the driveway leading to that gate.

Suddenly she made another realisation and it brought a swift rush of hope. *She was at the right hand* end of the house now. All she need do was slip around the end of the water butt and, keeping close to the wall, move along the side of the house well out of sight of the cheroot-smoker, until she found the drive.

Thank heaven she was still wearing her lavender day-gown. It would blend in well among the shadows as she moved. Lightly as some small wild creature hoping to escape detection, she crept forward. Just as she passed the corner of the house, a twig snapped under her foot. To Annabelle's tautened nerves, it sounded like the crack of a pistol shot.

''Ey, 'oo's that?'

Oh God, he had heard! Risking one look over her shoulder, she saw the red glimmer again, curving through the darkness as the man threw away his cheroot and started towards her. Grimshaw? It must be Grimshaw! That hoarse shout ... In a moment, he must see her. Where could she hide? There was no cover at all, nothing.

Annabelle kicked off her heeled shoes and ran.

There was nothing else she could do. Without her dainty high-heeled slippers, he might not hear her footsteps. Heart racing, she flew across the rough grass until her stockinged soles encountered gravel. Behind her she heard the man give another fierce shout. He must have seen her fleeing shadow!

With a gasp of terror, she rushed on, hardly aware of pain as her tender feet pressed the stony ground. Her one hope now was to prove more swift than he, escape into the dense darkness under the trees, hide and hope to evade him and discover the gateway.

The drive led away from the house through an avenue of trees. Beneath them, blackness lingered. She heard Grimshaw call out again: 'Hey! 'Oo's that? Stop! Come back 'ere! 'Ey, you ...'

She could not run any longer, the darkness was too thick. It was like moving into a blank wall. Nature rebelled with an instinctive shrinking, fearing injury. Hands outstretched before her, Annabelle stumbled along, judging the ground by the soreness in her soles, knowing that she made some noise panting for breath, but so desperate with fear that she could think of nothing other than to keep moving. Anything ... *anything* to prevent him catching her ... with his hands ...

She could not hear his boots crunching behind her. She became startlingly aware of the fact and stopped, listening, choking for breath, a stitch growing in her side. Between the tree-trunks she saw lights springing up in the house. So he had paused to alert the household! The extra seconds might yet spell her reprieve.

Soon, Gaspard as well as Grimshaw would be searching for her. Perhaps others too. She had no knowledge of whether anyone else was in the house; any other servants besides the Grimshaws. But she was certain of one thing. Gaspard would waste no time in going to check on her room!

She hurried on, assailed by a new fear. If she found the gates, suppose they were shut and barred? She might be trapped in these grounds. Were not large houses often surrounded by high walls? All at once, she perceived ahead a thinning of the darkness, a pale arc rising before her. She was coming to the end of the tree-tunnel, and the sky was brightening into day. Were the gates shut?

A few moments later, with unutterable thankfulness, she realised they were standing open. A small lodge-house stood beside the entrance, but its windows were dark. As she ran past she saw it was derelict, boarded up. Gaspard had said that the place had been unoccupied for years.

Out in the roadway, she realised she had no idea which way to turn to seek the town. A cool dawn breeze came to her from over the fields, smelling of sea-salt. She must make for the sea, and she must surely find the harbour eventually! She turned right and ran along the sloping track, stumbling in ruts. She was conscious now of the pain in her feet. Her white cotton stockings afforded little protection. Soon she would probably begin developing blisters and the agony would become acute.

She had gone about a hundred yards downhill when she felt the trembling reverberation of the ground under her soles. Galloping hooves! Horses were coming down the track behind her!

Annabelle glanced back, and her heart nearly stopped. They were hunting her with torches! With a cry of fright, she plunged instinctively for the hedge.

She had no recollection afterwards of getting through it. It was a thorn hedge and she felt her gown rip and the pain of scratching on her arms, but was not aware of the warm trickle of blood until later. In the field she crouched in the dewy grass of a ditch and heard the horses thunder by on the track. She was shaking violently, her breath coming in painful gasps, but they had not spotted her!

She dared not linger. She must get away before it dawned on them that she must have turned off the road, and they came back to search for her in the fields. She stared around. It was growing light rapidly now. She could see the black outlines of hedgerows, a silver rime of dew on the field, and way ahead, another glisten of silver. The sea!

She began to run again, blundering over the ruts of

a field lying fallow after last year's ploughing. Her stockinged feet were soaking, but it was much less painful crossing the field than it had been on the stony track. Her drenched skirts clung to her legs, hampering movement. She was grunting and heaving for breath, half weeping and praying silently, calling on the Virgin, and upon André, to help her.

She had struggled through another hedge and was halfway over a second field when she heard the distant shout behind her. Glancing back, she saw the flare of lights in the field; the first field she had crossed. They were following! She had been seen! What to do? She gazed all round, but there were no habitations in sight, no farmhouse or even a barn where she might contrive to hide. The sky was turning colour; rose pink and gold. The sun would soon rise, and the distant horizon of the sea glittered.

She noticed a five-barred gate ahead and ran towards it. She scarcely had enough strength left to pull herself up and over, weeping with terror; then the miracle happened. On the far side of the gate, regarding her with mild surprise, stood a gigantic coal-black carthorse.

Annabelle scrubbed the tears from her eyes and stared at it. She held out her hand, chirruping softly, pleadingly. The animal lowered its head and took an undecided pace in her direction, then blew noisily and continued cropping grass. Annabelle slid down from the gate. Her pursuers were in the field behind her now. She had, perhaps, two minutes. She approached the horse. It raised its head again, looking with no more than an expression of gentle curiosity at the dishevelled figure approaching. The girl went up to it, wound her fingers in its mane and urged it towards the gate.

She glimpsed two horsemen riding fast towards her over the adjoining meadow, then she had scrambled back on to the gate and flung herself, sprawling anyhow, on to the carthorse's broad back. She clung to its mane and urged it forward, kicking wildly at its glossy sides with her wet feet. The horse broke into a ponderous gallop.

Only sheer desperation kept Annabelle from falling off. With fingers twisted into its mane, she hung on for dear life, yelling at the great animal to 'Get on! Get on!' as it bumbled across the rough grass. She had to dismount to open another gate, and as she did so her two pursuers leapt the hedge behind her on their more agile steeds.

Annabelle half-pushed, half-pulled her massive charger through the gateway—and found herself in open country. They were on downland sloping towards the sea cliffs, but away to her right she saw a track, and then the roofs of houses ... Dover town!

Somehow she struggled back up on to her large mount and urged it along. They lolloped downhill and joined the track. At the foot of the hill, where the track became a footpath leading in among the cottages, she called her rescuer to a halt and looked back. Outlined against the hillside she could see her pursuers. They had stopped and were sitting motionless gazing down at her. So they had given up the chase!

With a sob of relief, Annabelle urged the carthorse along the path. She dared not dismount in case Gaspard or his servant took up the pursuit again. But now she felt comparatively safe. The carthorse clattered over the cobbles into the town.

Most of the town's inhabitants were still sleeping but one or two people were about. Annabelle became suddenly aware of what an extraordinary sight she must present; a wild girl in a torn gown, bare arms scratched and bleeding, hair hanging in wisps, sitting astride a giant black horse. No wonder folk were stopping to stare. She must resemble a gypsy woman. No one could recognise her for a lady. But she reflected that when she spoke, her voice must surely reveal her gentle breeding.

What ought she to do? She could stop at one of these houses and ask for help, but despite her past error and the fact that she was now beginning to shiver with chill from being so wet and from delayed shock, she was also experiencing such a glow of triumph at having outwitted the Marquis that it almost counteracted her discomforts.

A new thought had entered her mind. *The Swift!* Was the ship still in Dover harbour, and if so, was André aboard? Could the chance to discover finally whether he and Lockwood were one and the same person be almost within her grasp?

She would go down to the harbour, and if the sloop still rode at anchor, endeavour to persuade some fisherman to row her out to it.

Before she reached the harbour she saw the ship moored out in the bay, and her heart leapt with mixed hope and apprehension. Her determination was growing more inflexible each moment. She must know the truth about André. She could not wait another day to discover it. If he proved to be Lockwood she would not ask his aid, but she could count on the ship's skipper, Captain Strode, to assist her. That was the way in which she justified her reasoning to herself.

She had no money, no means whereby to purchase new garments, food and shelter. She must somehow bribe a fisherman, with promises of excellent payment, to take her out to *The Swift*, and then cast

herself upon the mercy of kindly Captain Strode. She
refused to face up to what the French captain, the
boat's true owner, would have to say about that.

More people were about in the street now, and
more than one fellow on his way to work shouted out
some ribald comment after the ragged girl riding
astride the huge horse. Annabelle held herself
proudly upright. One rough-looking young man in
fisherman's sweater and wool cap, shouted: 'Hey, my
beauty, late gettin' home? Gi' ye a penny for an hour
o' your time afore I go afloat?'

Annabelle, blushing with mortification at his impli-
cation, ignored him, urging the horse on. Reaching
the sea wall, she looked over and saw a number of
small fishing-boats by the quay. Some were piled with
freshly caught fish and their crews were busily unload-
ing the night's catch. She slid from her steed and stood
holding it by the mane, uncertain what to do with it.
She ought to return it to the field where she had found
it and reimburse its owner for the use she had had of it,
but lacking funds, she could not decide what to do.
She could not merely leave the horse wandering in the
town.

The first sun-rays glinted on the silver underbellies
of the dead fish. There were two or three rowing boats
pulled up above the tideline, but with no one in
attendance on them. She was considering hailing one
of the fishermen and imperiously demanding that he
should help her, when the clip-clop of hoofbeats on
the cobbles behind her made her start with renewed
fright and swing round. A single cloaked horseman
was riding towards her.

Annabelle stared in disbelief, gasped, then cried
out wildly: 'Monsieur Distel! Monsieur Distel! It is I,
Annabelle Sarne. *A moi*, *à moi!* Help me!'

CHAPTER
ELEVEN

THE young man gave a sharp exclamation and spurred his lathered horse to her side.

'Mademoiselle, what in heaven's name...?'

Now that real help was so miraculously within reach, Annabelle lost control. Laughing and crying as Distel swung himself out of the saddle, she let go of the carthorse's mane, and rushing to the secretary, clung to him shamelessly, pouring out an incoherent story.

'Oh, Monsieur Distel, how glad I am to see you ... How did you know? Oh, you have come to save me! I escaped ... knotted the sheets together.... I ran across fields, scrambled through hedges ... Oh, how did you know where to find me...?'

'Hush, Mademoiselle, please try to calm yourself,' he implored. But Annabelle was shivering and shaking, laughing hysterically while tears poured down her cheeks.

Gilbert Distel handled the situation with his customary efficiency. Grasping Annabelle's shoulders, he gave them a brisk shake, saying sharply, 'Be quiet at once, please,' then pulling off his cloak, wrapped it about the trembling girl.

'Now,' he said gently, 'try and tell me in a calm way what has happened to you.'

'I—I was abducted by that terrible man, my uncle's godson, the Marquis d'Hubert. Oh, Monsieur Distel, he—he took me to his house, somewhere near here, and had me locked in an upper room. He—he meant to seduce me, swore he would marry me...'

'*Mon Dieu!*'

'But I outwitted him,' Annabelle laughed, still inclined towards hysteria. 'I knotted sheets from the bed with my cloak and lowered myself from the window, only—only someone saw me and gave chase. I hid, then ran across some fields, but they came after me. The Marquis and his servant, I think. Then I saw this magnificent fellow,' indicating the carthorse still standing patiently beside the harbour wall. 'He saved me, but now,' she giggled hysterically again, 'I do not know what is to be done with him.'

'*Sacré bleu*, but what a tale!' Distel swore. 'Thank Our Lady you are safe. Do not fret any more. I shall attend to everything until such time as you can be restored to better hands than mine.'

'But *how* did you know where to seek for me?' Annabelle exclaimed again.

'I did not. 'Tis the purest good fortune that I have found you.'

'*What?* Then how do you come to be here?'

'Why, Mademoiselle, I have ridden most of the night since we discovered you had vanished. Suzanne went to see if you required anything, but you were not in your room. Nowhere could you be found, and there were signs of a carriage having been by the wall. Your poor mother has been distraught.'

'I was on my way to the chapel when a blanket was flung over my head and I was snatched up.'

He nodded. 'A horrifying experience, but it is over.'

'But, Monsieur, why are you here?' Annabelle repeated.

'I was coming to seek for Captain André and tell him we feared you had been kidnapped.'

'Oh ... Captain André?'

'Your safety is of much importance to him.' Distel paused. 'It was he who decided to make the arrangement, years ago, that I should enter the Comte's household, expressly in order to watch over you.'

'*What?*' gasped Annabelle.

'He has always shown the greatest interest in your welfare. I do not know his special reason...'

'I think I do,' Annabelle broke in, a trifle grimly. 'Monsieur Distel, I have made up my mind. I wish you to arrange at once for a boat to row us out to *The Swift*. I mean to see Captain André.'

Distel looked troubled.

'I do not know if he would wish...'

'I do not care whether he wishes to see me or not, I intend to see *him*. Do not look anxious. If you are still obliged to conceal his identity, it may surprise you to learn that I think I am aware of it. Monsieur Distel, your "French Captain" has expressed a wish to marry me.'

'*Marry* you?' It was the secretary's turn to look amazed.

'Yes, and it depends upon what transpires when I see him today whether I shall do so or not. So, Monsieur, I command you to take me out to *The Swift*.'

After a moment, Distel said, 'Very well, but you can hardly go as you are. I passed an inn but a short distance back. I suggest we go there, explain you have met with an accident, and see if we can obtain a fresh gown for you. Then you can rest and take some nourishment while I return here and arrange for a boat.'

'An excellent idea, but alas, I have no money!'

'I came well supplied. My horse is exhausted and

must rest and be groomed, and your fine steed will
need returning to its owner. Perhaps its absence from
the field has not yet been discovered.'

Annabelle felt less conspicuous wrapped in Distel's
cloak as they walked towards the inn, the secretary
leading both horses. In the inn-yard, an ostler came
hastily from the stables and Distel made arrangements for the carthorse to be taken home and its
owner paid for its use. The man stared with obvious
curiosity at Annabelle's torn and muddy stockings
peeping out from beneath the edge of the enveloping
cloak.

He must have thought them a peculiar pair of
people, the girl thought with inner amusement. Herself shoeless and untidy, and Distel, although he could
speak fluent English, still had a strong accent. When
they entered the inn, the landlord also eyed them
askance. On impulse, Annabelle turned to her companion.

'Monsieur Distel, I think it might be better to speak
all the truth.' She gave the suspicious-looking innkeeper her most bewitching smile. 'Sir, I am Miss
Annabelle Sarne of Sarne Manor. I must beg you to
keep this to yourself for the moment, but the truth is
that yesterday, I was abducted by two men and
brought to a house outside Dover. I managed to
escape from my captors, and by luck, encountered my
secretary Monsieur Distel, who had ridden here to
search for me.'

'Abducted, Miss?' repeated the landlord, managing
to appear scandalised and highly sceptical both at the
same time.

'I assure you, it is true. It—it was no common
kidnapping. The man who organised it had a particular reason, and I hope may eventually be brought to

justice. Meanwhile, I need a room for a few hours, food and rest, and if there is a woman in the house, loan of a clean gown. You shall be well paid, I promise you.'

As she spoke, Distel laid five gold guineas on the bar. The sight of the gold, plus Annabelle's voice and manner, must have convinced the man, for he began to bustle about, giving orders. Annabelle insisted that Distel must eat breakfast too before setting out again to see about the rowing-boat. Soon she was being ushered into a bedroom where a newly-lit fire flickered a welcome on the hearth, and the landlord's daughter stood waiting to maid her, a hip-bath prepared.

The girl exclaimed with shocked horror at sight of Annabelle's bruised feet. She was tall, but of the same slight build as Annabelle herself, and had brought one of her own gowns, a simple russet calico, to be tried on.

'But where are your shoes, Miss?' she cried, helping Annabelle out of her clothes. 'Mine'll never fit your little feet.'

'I—I lost them after the accident. I had to cross several fields, climb through hedges, before I could find a way to the town.'

'Oh, Miss! Was it a carriage accident?'

Annabelle chose to ignore this.

'Is there a cobbler's shop near here, and a haberdashery? If my man Distel gives you funds, could you go out and buy me fresh stockings and some soft slippers to wear?'

'I'm sure I could, Miss. There's shops just along the street from here.'

'I shall need a lightweight cloak too.'

'I've a brown summer cloak, Miss, nearly new.

You're welcome to that if it fits. Oh, your poor arms!
Let me bathe them scratches.'

'They are but surface scratches and will soon heal.
When you go out, if anyone inquires for a girl answer-
ing my description, I must ask you to say nothing.
Later, when I am gone from here, you may ask your
father to explain all to you. Have I your promise to
keep silent until then?'

The girl nodded, round-eyed with curiosity.

'You may comb out my hair now,' Annabelle told
her.

'Oh, Miss, I don't know how to dress a lady's hair.'

'No matter, I shall wear it loose. Have you a ribbon
I may thread through it as a bandeau to keep it in
place?'

By the time she was reclothed, Annabelle was not
dissatisfied by her appearance. The warm colour of
the russet gown suited her fair complexion. Her hair,
bound by pale blue ribbon, curled naturally against
her neck. Despite her simple attire, André surely
could not fail to think her pretty.

She had to remind herself that she was angry. If he
had been playing with her, using her....

She consumed an excellent breakfast, however,
of ham and eggs, toast and coffee, then sat resting
while she waited for Distel's return. The August
morning had clouded over and was becoming sultry,
but from the window she could observe that the sea
was glassily calm. *The Swift* had not moved from her
anchorage.

Annabelle felt nervous later, as the small rowing-boat
neared the sloop. Their approach had been noted, for
when she climbed aboard, Captain Strode was waiting
to greet her.

'Captain! Do you remember me? I am Annabelle Sarne.'

'Certainly I do, Miss.' If he felt surprise he showed none, but merely regarded her stolidly. Annabelle drew a quick breath.

'I—I have come to speak with Captain André. I trust he is still aboard?'

She noted the quick look the ship's captain shot at Gilbert Distel, who nodded.

'Come this way, if you please, Ma'am. I'll have the gentleman summoned.'

'Wait for me here, please, Monsieur Distel. I must see Captain André alone,' she whispered, and followed Strode down the companionway. He showed her into the saloon.

'If you'll be seated, Miss Sarne?'

But now Annabelle was too restless and anxious to relax. In a moment, she would know the truth. A wild hope still lingered, refusing to be entirely quenched, that it would be her true lover who came to her now to resolve all her fears, but when the door opened and she saw Marcus Lockwood on the threshold, it was with no sense of shock. She was aware only of an aching sadness. It was true, then. He had tried to use her. She could not trust his words of love.

For a tense moment they stood regarding each other in silence, then he came forward to lean with his hands on the table's edge.

'Annabelle, why are you here?'

She swallowed, then drawing on her reserve of Camoret pride, drew herself upright and faced him bravely.

'I came, sir, to discover whether my suspicions regarding you were true. I find that they are.'

After a moment, he said: 'I imagine you are

extremely angry. Perhaps you have a right, but if you will bear with me, hear what I have to tell you . . .'

'There seems small point in my remaining here a second longer,' she broke in. 'I—I think the position is plain, sir.' Despite herself, her voice began to shake. 'You—you must have found my—swift response to your blandishments excessively amusing. I must suppose you imagined that once having fallen under your spell, I should not have had the strength to break free, Major Marcus Lockwood, Major Cheat and Liar!'

She saw his mouth tighten, but his eyes, those strangely beautiful golden hazel eyes, were full of sadness.

'Annabelle,' he said quietly, 'don't. I love you.'

The gentle sorrow of his expression brought her up short, but all the disillusionment, fear and misery she had suffered on his account was welling inside her. She could not stop.

'Love me?' she cried with passionate scorn. 'Rather I think you love the wealth of my Sarne estate, the inheritance I should have if I were foolish enough to marry you. Marry a rich heiress! That is the way, is it not, in which many an adventurer has bought back a lost position in society?'

'Society?' He gave a curt, mirthless laugh. 'I can assure you that I care not a fig for that false world. I soon found who were my true friends when my father fell from grace and I had to pay his debts. As I once said to you, I think that neither of us has much reason to be proud of our fathers and what they did for us.'

'You do not deny that you had Gilbert Distel plant himself at Camoret to keep an eye on me while I finished my growing up in France? To keep an eye on the goose who would one day lay the golden eggs? Oh,

I have been goose indeed to think I might trust the mysterious French captain!' Annabelle cried angrily, and had the satisfaction of seeing him bite his lip.

Then he said gently: 'I do not deny that at first I did intend to follow the course mapped for us by our fathers, to marry you for gain. Distel's task at Camoret was to watch over you—my investment for the future!' His smile was bitter and painfully crooked. 'But I reckoned without one thing, Annabelle Sarne. I never dreamed that when I saw you for myself, I should fall in love. Oh yes. I swear to you that I fell on sight. That was no lie. I loved you, as I told you, from the time I saw you in that carriage, looking so small and scared but determined to be brave and defend your mother and Mademoiselle Dupont if you could.'

Annabelle gazed at him.

'I—I—how can I believe you? When you came to Sarne as your real self, you gave me no inkling.'

'How could I? It was essential that no hint of a connection between the English major and the French captain should be suspected by anyone, not even you. I was shortly returning to France to try and rescue your uncle the Comte. I knew you must hate the name of Lockwood, and I could see that you did. *That* was no time for explanations.'

'But—but you came to me again, that very same night,' she whispered. 'On the bridge, you came as André...'

'And vowed my love for you, which was true. I begged you to trust me. I had to see you once more before leaving for Paris, to learn if there was any hope that one day you might love me as I already knew I loved and wanted you. I thought that if I helped your uncle it might tell in my favour once you discovered my true identity. Yes, I had a selfish reason for aiding that particular nobleman. I admit the fact now.'

'You *did* save him. He is safe at Sarne. For that I must thank you, at least,' she murmured breathlessly.

He took a step towards her, but she drew back.

'Annabelle,' he pleaded, 'can you not forgive me? Can you not believe that I do love you? I swear that, by all that I hold holy.'

'Do you hold *anything* holy?'

He met her look steadily.

'I do. I swore a vow that I would aid the wrongfully oppressed, and I have kept that vow. I have told you why I concealed certain facts from you. I implore your understanding. I freely admit that before I met you, I meant to marry you to gain your wealth, to aid me in my schemes of work in France, but now I shall take nothing from you unless you give it by your own desire. If you will not marry me because you cannot love me, then I shall never claim Sarne from you. All that is in the past. You are entirely free to choose.'

Suddenly, she smiled. Her whole face lit with so much joy that he caught his breath in amazement.

'Oh, André, my love, I do believe you now! You have set me free.'

In two strides he had come round the table and pulled her into his arms. Neither could speak in those first rapturous moments as they clung together.

At last, with his cheeks against her hair, he murmured: 'My darling, my little love, I have been so afraid I might lose you altogether once you found I was Lockwood. When did you suspect it?'

'When my uncle arrived at Sarne and described the captain who had hoodwinked the French prison authorities. He spoke of his rescuer's unusual eyes. I felt sure two men could not have eyes of such an exceptional golden hazel shade.'

'My poor sweetheart! These wretched eyes of mine have nearly proved my downfall on more than one occasion. I hoped I might return to explain myself before you received any hint, but I have been detained here until now.'

'So Distel said. He is here with me now.'

'Strode informed me. I hope he has been taking proper care of you?' He held her at arms' length and she saw a puzzled look come into his face. 'You look—different, Annabelle. You are dressed very simply for the Mistress of Sarne, almost like a country wench. Is there a purpose? Have you travelled here incognito for some reason?'

'No, André, but these are not my clothes! I suppose I had better tell you it all. Let us sit together on this settle, for it is a long tale and will take some telling.'

She commenced her story, and he listened in silence until she began describing her abduction, then Lockwood swore under his breath and his arm tightened about her shoulders.

'By God, d'Hubert shall pay for this! My sweet love, are you harmed at all?'

'No, I am not, save for a few scratches where I had to scramble in the hedgerows to conceal myself,' she assured him, smiling ruefully. 'It was a terrifying experience, climbing from that upper storey window, but I am quite delighted with myself for having achieved such a venture without mishap.'

'You might have killed yourself! What madcap courage! I would hardly have thought you capable of such a desperate undertaking.'

'I did it only because I *was* desperate. I had to

rescue myself or succumb.' And she shivered briefly at
the recollection.

'That villain shall be made to pay dearly for causing
you one second's anguish,' Lockwood vowed. 'Had I
realised the depth of his cunning and wickedness, I
would not have left you unguarded, even at Sarne.'

'André, I am terrified of what may happen if you
meet. Gaspard has sworn to kill you. He—he is a
brilliant swordsman.'

'I am not feeble myself when it comes to swordplay,
but he does not merit that honour reserved for
gentlemen. A sound horse-whipping is what he
deserves, and what he will get if he is foolhardy
enough to cross my path. Don't look so frightened,
love, it may not even come to that, more's the pity.
D'Hubert is an attempted murderer. He planned your
uncle's death. At the very least, I shall obtain his
banishment from England.'

'Have you the power to achieve that?' she asked,
gazing at him in wonder.

'I believe so. I may tell you this now, as my work in
France is finished for the moment. Even so, you must
keep it in confidence.'

'Tell me what, André?'

'I have been acting as an agent for the English army.
I am—well acquainted with a number of men in high
government positions. There is a growing fear that
war with France cannot be long postponed. It has
been part of my task to discover what I could regarding the imminence of trouble; of certain French plans.
My work aiding French *emigrés* was partly cover,
although I myself developed an immense interest in
it.'

'War with France?' she repeated, paling. In the
midst of her new happiness with him she could think

of nothing but his personal safety.

'Don't be anxious. As I have said, my work in France is finished for the nonce. I may even leave the army and settle down to life as an English country gentleman, once we are married,' he added, half teasingly, and then with complete seriousness: 'Annabelle, the important question now is: "When will you marry me?"'

She looked up at him shyly, but laughing a little.

'I am shameless enough to reply, sir, "As soon as you wish."'

'If you mean that, my darling, then it can be today.'

'Today?' she echoed.

'We are at sea. Captain Strode has the power to make us man and wife. Shall I give orders for him to weigh anchor and take us out into mid-Channel? Will you dare all, and marry me now? Give me full right to defend you against all comers so that d'Hubert, *no one*, will dare touch you?'

Looking up into his smiling, eager eyes, Annabelle experienced such an uprush of happiness that she felt almost faint, but she said slowly: 'I cannot refuse you, for I love you more than all the world, and trust you completely now. But—but can you understand this? Captain Strode may make us legal man and wife, but I fear I shall not feel entirely married in the sight of God without the blessing of my Church.'

'I admit to you that I do not own strong religious views. I believe that it cannot matter in which capacity one worships God, but I understand your feelings,' Lockwood said. 'Tomorrow we will go back to Sarne and repeat our vows in your chapel. Father Martin shall bless our union.'

'Oh please, André! Then I shall be perfectly happy.'

.   .   .   .

Lockwood and Annabelle were married that evening by the ship's captain with two of the crew as witnesses. Distel left the sloop once he had been told of the plan, to go back to Sarne and assure Annabelle's family of her wellbeing, and prepare for the homecoming. At the brief wedding ceremony on the deck of the ship, she learned, for the first time, that her husband's full name was Marcus Andrew Lockwood.

'But I shall never call you anything other than André,' she declared afterwards. 'I cannot think of you in any other way. It is the name by which I first came to love you. Mama will be quite enchanted that I have married the English Major after all. Mama,' she added, looking slightly worried, 'owns a Frenchwoman's practical eye for the main chance, I'm afraid. Rather than lose Sarne, she was wholly prepared to let me sacrifice myself and marry you, Major Lockwood, sir, if by doing so, I could keep my riches. But I can forgive her now,' smiling so that he could not resist kissing her again.

'*My* mother and sisters will love you, I know, and welcome you as my wife,' he declared.

That night, lying in his arms, rocked by the gentle motion of the ship and warmed by his kisses, Annabelle found it possible to forget all her past troubles; even the smothered fear that somehow, the Marquis d'Hubert might still contrive a means to do them harm.

CHAPTER
TWELVE

Lockwood and Annabelle set out for Sarne in the early afternoon of the following day. He had wanted to take her on a shopping expedition, buy her a complete new outfit in which to travel home, and return the borrowed cloak and gown to the innkeeper's daughter, but morning brought a return of Annabelle's fears. She dreaded a meeting with either the Marquis or his servant Grimshaw in the town, although Lockwood was sceptical of the possibility.

'D'Hubert must know that he has committed a serious crime by abducting you. He probably expected swift retribution and has left the district already. Very likely, he will quit this country without delay.'

'But he does not know that my uncle and Monsieur Distel are safe and in England! He thinks my mother and I are without male protection, and naturally he does not know that *you* are here in Dover. Oh, please let us go straight home, André. At Sarne the servants have orders not to allow him entrance. I shall feel much safer there, and neither do I want him to meet *you*. We can return the garments lent to me and send further remuneration by messenger.'

'Very well, my love, if that is what you want, but I doubt we shall ever hear more of d'Hubert. He has shot his bolt, and must surely reckon his safest course to be a swift disappearance.'

However, Lockwood refused to leave Dover

without first reporting the whole affair to the local constable, and went ashore accompanied by one of the ship's officers, leaving Annabelle in Strode's care. While in the town, he told her, he could also arrange for the hire of a carriage to convey her home. His horse was stabled at another of the town's hostelries, and he would ride beside her carriage in case they met with trouble from footpads on the way. The journey back to Surrey would take several hours; they might even be forced to spend a night en route.

Annabelle endured a restless and agitated morning. Despite her husband's reassurances, she felt that d'Hubert might still be a source of danger, and she almost wept with relief when at last she saw the rowing-boat returning with Lockwood and the officer on board. She felt quite sorry at having to bid farewell to Captain Strode and *The Swift*. On board she had felt secure, wholly beyond d'Hubert's reach. Strode would be leaving Dover on the evening tide to sail round to the Thames.

Lockwood told Annabelle that soon after their return to Sarne, he must spend a few days in Town to clear up some business matters, but she could go with him if she chose. She declared that she would. She felt that she could not bear any further separation from him at present.

Their journey to Sarne went off without incident, and it was late evening when the carriage finally turned in at the Manor gates. The Comte and Solange, Distel and Suzanne came out on to the steps to greet them. Solange, weeping with joy, folded Annabelle in an embrace.

'My beloved child, all thanks to Our Blessed Lady for keeping you safe! Dear Monsieur Distel has told us everything that befell you. Imagine my tortures of anxiety! Even my dear brother could think of no words to bring me any comfort. Suzanne and I have both been wholly distraught.'

'But Mama, surely Monsieur Distel told you also that I am quite unharmed, and now so extremely happy? Mama, and my dearest uncle, let me introduce my husband to you.'

'I am amazed, enthralled!' cried Solange, pink chins a-quiver, and clasping André's hand in both her own soft plump ones. 'My son-in-law, welcome! To think that you are Annabelle's French captain, but also the English major! Everything has resolved itself quite beautifully.'

'I trust you are not angry that our marriage has taken place in such a clandestine manner?' Lockwood said. 'It seemed the best course, as your daughter and I both wished for it, giving me the right to defend her upon all occasions.'

'My dear sir, it is the perfect solution!' exclaimed the Comte de Camoret, wringing his hand. 'And now I can at last thank you for my own salvation.'

'Oh, that wicked, evil man, Gaspard!' Solange cried. 'Annabelle, how petrified with fear you must have been! I can scarcely wait to hear every single detail of what passed.'

They all stayed up most of the night talking, for naturally Solange and the Comte wanted to hear it all from Annabelle's own lips. Suzanne and Distel remained in the drawing-room with them, and Annabelle was happy to note that her mother's attitude towards the pair had warmed considerably.

'We owe Gilbert so much,' Solange said, smiling at him. Gilbert! Annabelle thought. So he had been promoted to the status of family friend! 'Thank heaven he found you and was able to take you immediately to Major Lockwood. Oh, la la, I have not been so thrilled for years, although it saddens me to think I could not attend my only daughter's wedding.'

' 'Twas but a civil ceremony, Mama. In a few days' time we plan another in the chapel here, so that we may receive Father Martin's blessing.'

'Then why not make it a double ceremony?' the Comte remarked. 'Distel and Mademoiselle Dupont also hope to marry very shortly.'

This suggestion appeared to charm everyone concerned.

'I have yet one more surprise to impart,' Annabelle told them. 'It seems that our dear Father Martin is the nominal head of the organisation to which André and Gilbert belong.'

'He was the instigator of the whole idea,' Lockwood added. 'He has been much concerned for the safety of priests and others in France since the troubles began in July '89 when the Bastille prison fell. He planned our forays; I was asked to act as leader in the field of operations.'

'It seems that much has been going on here during our absence, Mama,' Annabelle said, 'but now, André will be remaining in England.' She gazed adoringly at her husband. 'I could not bear to let him go back to such danger at the moment.'

'Certainly for the present I shall stay here,' Lockwood nodded, lifting her hand to his lips. 'We must wait to see what turn events take next, but that is in the future and need not trouble us tonight.'

'Much as it saddens me, I cannot help but hope that d'Hubert will be found and brought to justice,' exclaimed the Comte de Camoret.

·   ·   ·   ·   ·

Some days later, a messenger arrived from Dover, bringing news that the house Annabelle had described had been located. There were signs of recent habitation, but no one was there. Her grey cloak and the knotted sheets were still inside the water-butt and so bore out her story.

'Obviously the vultures have flown,' Lockwood remarked. 'Now, my dearest wife, I hope you will no longer feel afraid when I am not with you.'

That day, when Annabelle came downstairs, she saw a new footman crossing the hall, carrying a tray of bottles and glasses with which to replenish the drawing-room wine table. He was a young fresh-faced lad of about her own age, and he blushed awkwardly when he saw her.

'Oh, I—I beg pardon, Miss, er—Ma'am, er—Milady . . .'

'Ma'am will do very well,' Annabelle told him, smiling. 'You are new here, are you not? What is your name?'

'Robin, Ma'am. I only started yesterday.'

'Where is your home? Are you from the village?'

'I come from Farnham way. Mr Proudfoot is my grand-uncle.'

'I see. Well, I hope you will be very happy working here, Robin.'

She passed on into the morning-room and forgot him, never dreaming that very shortly he was to prove the instrument of near-disaster.

The double wedding ceremony in the chapel was scheduled for the following afternoon. The Sarne seamstress had been busy working overtime, fashioning a new satin gown for her young mistress to wear; Suzanne had elected to make her own wedding dress of white organza. She and Annabelle were putting the finishing touches to it by embroidering daisy-petals about the neckline. After the midday meal they sat in the drawing-room, stitching busily, while Solange rested on the couch, watching lazily. Lockwood and Distel had gone with the Comte to Winkworth Grange, to be shown Mr Francis Trecarey's collection of snuff-boxes, and would be bringing their neighbour back to dine at Sarne and spend the evening at the manor.

Solange had entirely made up her mind. Although Mr Trecarey did not yet know it himself, he would soon be proposing marriage to her. Annabelle was a married woman now; Sarne had a new master. Solange was extremely pleased, but she had come to realise that she no longer wanted to play second fiddle to her daughter. Henri had expressed an intention of setting up a small establishment in Town and thought she might like to join him there, but fond as she was of her twin brother, and grateful for his past care of her, Solange had decided that to become mistress of Winkworth Grange would be infinitely preferable. She could see no reason why the achievement of this simple ambition should be long delayed. Dear Mr Trecarey was already her devoted slave. It was purely a matter of time, and preparing the ground for the correct moment!

A tap on the drawing-room door and it opened to reveal the new young footman, Robin. He addressed himself to Annabelle.

'If you please, Mrs Lockwood, Ma'am, there is a gentleman to see you.' He stepped aside, and red-faced with pride at his new-found importance, announced clearly and in appalling French: 'Moun-seer le Marquis de Hubert.'

Solange started up, uttered a stifled screech, and

swooned back on the couch. Dropping her embroidery needle, Annabelle rose, staring at the door as though mesmerised, while Suzanne, with an exclamation, sprang to her feet and rushed to stand beside her friend as if ready to defend her.

Gaspard, Marquis d'Hubert, exquisite in every sartorial detail, entered the room. Annabelle might have been forgiven for thinking she faced a wraith, for he was clothed entirely in shades of palest grey; grey hat, powdered wig, grey-caped topcoat, pearl-grey hessians. The only deviation from this portrait in ash occurred in the cold blue glitter of his eyes, and in the dull glow of a ruby amid the froth of grey lace at his throat. Even his walking cane was grey, topped by a knob of polished gold. Monsieur le Marquis swept the three petrified ladies a deep and elegant bow.

'Annabelle, vision of beauty!' he murmured in languid tones. 'Dear Aunt Solange! But what ails my godmother? Has she fainted?'

No one answered. The two girls stood gazing at him in horror-stricken silence. D'Hubert raised delicately pencilled brows.

'Come, *ma chère* Annabelle, are you not going to offer me a seat and some refreshment? I have had a most tedious journey from Town. Indeed, a tedious time of it in the whole three weeks since last we met! I have searched high and low for that impudent rascal, Lockwood, in order to call him out and teach him a lesson, but nowhere is he to be found.'

Annabelle regained the use of her voice.

'Three weeks?' she repeated. 'I—I what can you mean? Who allowed you in here? I gave instructions—oh, 'twas that new lad, I suppose. He cannot have known ... How dare you return here now, after what you did—tried to do to me—barely a week since?'

D'Hubert surveyed her, an expression of mild astonishment on his face. It was, Annabelle realised in dazed fashion, a most consummate piece of acting, of attempted bluff.

'A week since? My dearest girl, of what are you speaking? It is all of three weeks since our—conversation here. I refer, naturally, to the discussion of our future.'

'*I* refer, sir, to your abduction of me exactly eight days ago; my imprisonment in that house outside Dover, and your threats to force me into marriage! I trust you were astonished by the manner in which I succeeded in outwitting you?'

The Marquis uttered a small, bored yawn. 'What an extraordinary statement! Totally incomprehensible to me. Abduction? House at Dover? I cannot understand what is your possible meaning.'

Solange, finding that no one was exhibiting the least concern over her, opened her eyes and sat up slowly, pressing a kerchief to her lips. Gaspard made her a slight leg.

'You do not appear overjoyed to see me, Godmother. Can *you* explain this arrant nonsense Annabelle is talking?'

Solange merely made a choking sound, her eyes bulging with fright.

'Suzanne,' Annabelle spoke sharply, 'kindly ring the bell at once.' Her eyes never left the Marquis's.

As Suzanne took a nervous step in the direction of the bell-rope, he said softly, but with such a note of menace in his voice that she stopped with a jerk: 'I should not, if I were you, summon the servants as yet, Mademoiselle Dupont. First I think we will extract a promise from Mademoiselle Sarne, before witnesses, to honour the agreement her uncle the Comte de Camoret made with me. Namely, that she shall agree to become my wife without any further waste of time.'

'That is a promise she might find difficult to keep,' Lockwood spoke with deadly quiet from the doorway, 'seeing that the lady already possesses a husband.'

D'Hubert whipped round. 'Husband?'

'I, sir, own that inestimable honour. Major Marcus Andrew Lockwood, at your service,' and he sketched a slight, wholly insulting, mockery of a bow.

Annabelle heard the indrawn hiss of d'Hubert's breath. As Lockwood stepped across the threshold, with Distel immediately behind him, the Marquis moved back a pace so that he formed the apex of a triangle between the two men and the three frightened women, but his way of exit was cut off.

'So,' he said softly, after a moment. 'You are he; the insolent scallywag of an Englishman who dares to insult the name of d'Hubert.'

'Gaspard, he is my husband,' Annabelle said quietly, and held out her left hand. On the third finger, the gold of Lockwood's signet ring still glinted. Tomorrow he would have exchanged it for a more conventional plain gold wedding band.

The Marquis swore beneath his breath. His face had grown ashen, two patches of furious colour on his cheekbones.

'I think, Monsieur le Marquis, you had best concede defeat,' Lockwood remarked. He stood rocking lightly on his heels, but the expression in his golden eyes made Annabelle catch her breath with fear. 'I know the extent of evil to which you are prepared to go,' Lockwood continued quietly. 'You planned the legalised murder of the Comte de Camoret. My friend

Distel, here, can testify to that. You have offered threats and abuse to myself. But of far greater importance to *me*, you have dared to lay hands upon the lady who is now my wife, causing her fear and anguish. So it will be my personal pleasure to give you the thrashing you deserve. Afterwards the constables can lock you in the common gaol, for aught I care, until such time as you stand trial for breaking English law by abducting Annabelle and holding her against her will. Distel, call the servants! Have him hog-tied and removed to the stable yard, his natural place, where presently I shall attend on him with my horse-whip.'

Gaspard d'Hubert made an inarticulate sound in his throat. Something flashed upward, and in an instant, the gold-topped cane in his hand had changed its character to become a deadly weapon. A wicked-looking stem of glistening steel shot from its tip and quivered in the air, pointing straight at Lockwood's heart. Annabelle screamed, then Distel shouted: 'By God, you would attack an unarmed man!'

He launched himself past Lockwood, coming at d'Hubert from the side, fists clenched and flailing. It was a mad, courageous, hopeless gesture. Steel flashed; blood spurted against the wall. With a cry Suzanne sprang forward, brushing by the Marquis regardless of his weapon, and caught Distel in her arms as he staggered back, clutching at his shoulder. D'Hubert spun on his heel as Lockwood sprang at him—and the Comte de Camoret walked calmly through the doorway, followed by Mr Francis Trecarey.

D'Hubert's mouth fell open. In that second of ludicrous shock Lockwood was on him and had twisted the swordstick from his grasp, and Gaspard, Marquis d'Hubert, found himself flattened against the wall, the point of his own steel pricking the base of his throat.

'Heaven above, what is going on here?' exclaimed the Comte, while Mr Trecarey hurried to bend solicitously over Solange, who had fainted in earnest this time and slipped sideways on the couch. Suzanne was on her knees, tearing strips from her petticoat to press on Distel's wound.

'This *canaille* was trying to kill me,' Lockwood said coolly, over his shoulder. 'If you please, Camoret, summon the servants.'

In a matter of moments, the room was filled with people, D'Hubert, his face contorted with fury and despair, hands pinioned behind him, was hustled away, none too gently, by several men. Annabelle flung herself into her husband's arms.

Lockwood kissed her tenderly, then put her aside. 'Wait, my dearest. First, I must attend to Distel.'

'Oh yes, yes, André! Quickly, help Suzanne!'

Lockwood knelt down and examined the deep slash under Distel's collar-bone, then made a swift neat pad of the rest of Suzanne's underskirt.

'There, my friend, you will live to try such foolhardy acts of bravery on other occasions, if you so wish. Dry your tears, Mademoiselle Suzanne, he'll be none the worse for this blood-letting. 'Tis not so bad and missed the artery by a full half-inch. Camoret, a glass of brandy for the patient, if you will be so kind. He does look a trifle green about the gills. Annabelle, send that new young numbskull of a footman out to fetch the doctor. He may as well try and justify his existence in some way. Trecarey, how does my mother-in-law? Is she recovering from her shock of fright?'

An hour or so later, serenity was restored to the house. Gilbert Distel, his shoulder expertly bound by the physician, lay resting on the drawing-room sofa, Suzanne on a stool at his side. Lockwood and Annabelle had already given their account of the affair to the sheriff; Solange, the Comte, and Trecarey were in process of describing theirs. D'Hubert had been taken away in a closed carriage. He had admitted everything, stating that he had paid off his accomplices, the Grimshaws, and sent them back to 'the rat holes they came from in London' after Annabelle's escape from the house near Dover. The law would seek them in Town.

While waiting for the sheriff to complete his inquiries, Lockwood and Annabelle wandered out into the garden. Without either actually making the suggestion, they moved in accord towards the woodland path leading to the chapel. On the little iron bridge they paused, and stood gazing down into the glistening ripples of water coursing beneath it. Lockwood had his arm closely about her, and her head rested against his shoulder.

'I can scarcely believe that it is all over and you are quite unscathed,' the girl murmured. 'Oh, André, I have been so frightened for your safety! Gaspard made such terrible threats against you.'

'*You* were in far greater danger than I, my love, but now you have nothing more to fear.'

Annabelle shivered.

'Until his release. Then he might attempt revenge once more.'

' 'Tis most unlikely he will win back freedom for many years. If and when that happens, he will be banished from England; have no fear on that score.' He paused. 'I am still at something of a loss to understand his motive for hating your uncle so much.'

Annabelle hesitated, then she said:

'I have spoken with Uncle Henri and he has given his permission for me to tell you everything. He, not the Duc, is Gaspard's real father.'

Lockwood whistled his astonishment.

'You mean his mother, the Duchesse...?'

Annabelle nodded.

'Perhaps we should feel some pity for Gaspard in spite of what he has tried to do to us. I think hē did love his mother, and like all French boys of noble family, was brought up to believe passionately in the honour and pride of his name. He is arrogant by nature, too, and it must have been an appalling shock to learn that he had no more than a legal right to that name, and that his adored mother had been unfaithful to her husband.'

'I suppose it must, although affairs of the heart outside marriage are not so rare amongst the nobility.'

'The Marquis had led a sheltered boyhood, spending much time alone with his mother. Poor lady, she was very unhappy,' Annabelle murmured.

'How so?'

'The Duc was much older than she, and, so my uncle declares, a drunken sot even at the time she married him—she was forced to do so by her parents. He was cruel to her, and my uncle, unfortunately, was not happy with his own wife.'

'That,' said Lockwood, kissing her, 'is often the fate of marriages made for convenience.'

Annabelle smiled faintly.

'My uncle and the Duchesse fell deeply in love, but naturally, it was hopeless, doomed to end in tragedy for someone. Gaspard became very bitter towards his mother once he knew the truth. He has no compassion in his nature. He told me that he thinks love is for sentimental fools.'

'Does he, indeed?' asked Lockwood, and kissed her again. 'Then it is he who is the fool.'

'There is one small thing that still puzzles me, André, and perhaps *you* can supply the answer.'

'What is that, sweetheart?'

'The night before Mama and Suzanne and I fled from France, I saw Gilbert Distel in the château garden, speaking with a man muffled in a cloak. I could not see the man's face, but they seemed to wish not to be observed.'

Lockwood grinned.

'I think you have guessed correctly. It was I.'

'Gilbert told me you had arranged for him to watch over me while I lived in France, but as you know, I feared it was because you wanted an eye kept on the goose who might one day lay the golden eggs.'

This time, Lockwood laughed outright and kissed the tip of her nose.

'We disposed of that point on our wedding day aboard ship. But to revert to my meeting with Distel, yes, I had a regular rendezvous with him so that he could report on any matters of importance. That night he told me he feared the Comte might soon be in grave danger. He warned me that the Marquis d'Hubert had been sounding him out on the chances of bribing him to betray the Comte. I assured him that *The Swift* would be waiting to carry you all away safely to England should the need arise—which it did, the very next day. Unfortunately, it was sooner than I had anticipated.'

'Yes.' She leaned closer against him. 'It may take me—a little time to feel perfectly secure again.'

'I know. I understand, my darling. But I shall be with you from now on. I shall take care of you always.'

'My beloved French captain!' She looked up at him, laughing a little, tenderly.

'Yes, Annabelle,' he answered seriously, and lifted her hand to hold against his cheek. 'We do belong to each other completely now, and tomorrow, when we repeat our marriage vows before Father Martin, we shall receive God's blessing on our union.'

His mouth came down on hers once more.

'My beautiful wife,' he murmured against her lips, 'you need never feel afraid again. To me, you are more precious than my own life.'

Feeling the strength of his arms around her, the warmth and passion of his kisses, Annabelle's last remnants of fear melted away. She reached up, slipping her arms about his neck and pressing against him so that her body seemed to fuse with his in tenderness and joy that she knew would last their lifetime together.

Masquerade
Historical Romances

Intrigue
excitement
romance

Don't miss
November's
other enthralling Historical Romance title

LADY IN THE LION'S DEN
by Elaine Reeve

Kidnapped and held as a hostage by the Saxon lion, Leowulf, lord of Erinwald ... The proud Norman lady Adela de Lise refuses to submit to such rough treatment. Defying her captor at every turn, she fights furiously for her freedom, and her right to return in peace to Normandy at the side of her beloved Guy de Brec.

But to Leowulf, Adela is the means to make his peace with William of Normandy, King and conqueror of his country. He will do anything to force Adela to stay with him — even if it means making her his wife ...

Masquerade
Historical Romances

Intrigue excitement romance

A PERFECT MATCH
by Julia Murray

Louisa married Simon, Lord Winslow, very reluctantly indeed, and she knew that he had only offered for her to preserve the proprieties. So why should he interfere with her innocent attempts to help his unhappy brother-in-law, Henry Landry?

FRENCHMAN'S HARVEST
by Emma Gayle

Helen Caister agreed to visit her mother's old home – a château in the Médoc region of France – only because she had fallen in love with her cousin, Marc d'Auray, and could not refuse his invitation. But Marc cared only for his inheritance and his precious vines . . .

Look out for these titles in your local paperback shop from
12th December 1980

Masquerade
Historical Romances

Intrigue excitement romance

TARRISBROKE HALL
by Jasmine Cresswell

Utter ruin confronted the Earl of Tarrisbroke. Faced with discharging his father's mountainous gambling debts, what could he do but marry for money? But the wife he chose, the wealthy young widow Marianne Johnson, was not at all the vulgar title-hunting woman he expected!

ZULU SUNSET
by Christina Laffeaty

Cassandra Hudson wanted to be a missionary's wife — more particularly, her cousin Martin's wife. So she travelled to Zululand to visit him, confident that her new fortune would smooth her way. Unfortunately she found herself in the midst of an impending war between whites and Zulus, and the only man who could help her reach Martin was the odious, arrogant Saul Parnell . . .

These titles are still available through your local paperback retailer